4

THE GIRLS OF CANBY HALL®

KEEPING SECRETS

EMILY CHASE

SCHOLASTIC INC.

New York Toronto London Auckland Sydney

ISBN 0-590-40081-9

12 11 10 9 8 7 6 5 4 3   6 7 8/8

Printed in the U.S.A.   01

THE GIRLS
OF CANBY HALL®

KEEPING
SECRETS

Printed in the U.S.A.

THE GIRLS OF CANBY HALL®

CHAPTER ONE

"You've been studying that list forever, Faith," Dana Morrison observed as she experimented with various ways of wearing a multicolored shawl that her mother had just sent her from New York. Dana had striking good looks — long brown hair, green eyes, a model-like figure — that matched her magnetic personality. Her two roommates, Faith Thompson and Shelley Hyde, both agreed that it didn't matter what Dana wore. She could make a potato sack look chic.

"Yeah," Shelley piped up. "You act as though you expect to receive some message from outer space." Shelley, blond, blue-eyed, and cherubic was sitting cross-legged on the floor, knitting a sleeve of the pink cardigan sweater that she planned to give her mother for her birthday.

"This is almost as hopeless as expecting to hear from E.T." Faith laughed.

"What, exactly, are you doing?" Dana asked.

Faith had stretched her tall, slender frame against the propped-up pillows of her madras-covered bed and peered above her wire-framed reading glasses at Dana. "I've got to find someone to take pictures for the 'Historic Homes of Boston' story by next week. It's for the June issue of the *Clarion.*"

Faith was the star photographer for the Canby Hall newspaper and took her job seriously, loving every minute of it.

"Why the list?" Shelley inquired.

"This gives all the names and addresses of the Canby Hall girls. Whoever covers the story should know the area and something about taking pictures. I've narrowed it down to those who live in Boston or within a fifteen-mile radius."

"Who does that leave?"

"According to my requirements, Mary Beth Grover is the best candidate."

"Mary Beth!" Dana exclaimed. She had draped the shawl around her like a sarong and was twirling around in front of the full-length mirror that hung on the front of the closet door. She stopped in mid-twirl, as though she'd been splashed with a bucket of cold water.

"You've got to be kidding," Shelley said.

"M.B. was one of the first kids in this school I tried to be friendly with, and I think more than anything else was one of the reasons I had an almost fatal bout with homesickness last semester."

They all recalled how Shelley had confided, after the three of them had ironed out their difficulties and become so tight — the laundry-room story. Shelley, who was super neat, did her laundry at least three times a week and usually at odd hours. It was the first week of school and Shelley had gone into the laundry room before breakfast. She was waiting for the dry cycle to be completed when Mary Beth appeared and silently dumped her clothes into a washing machine, not even acknowledging Shelley's presence. After what seemed like an endless period of uncomfortable silence, Shelley, half-kidding, and in her ingenuous small-town manner, asked Mary Beth which laundry soap she thought was the best.

"How would I know?" Mary Beth had responded, unsmilingly. "It's not something I experiment with."

Shelley was so taken aback by her abrupt answer that she grabbed her clothes, which were still damp, and bolted out of the laundry room before Mary Beth (who Shelley then dubbed M.B. — Mean Bean) could see she was on the verge of tears. They were tears of anger, more than hurt, because she didn't know how to handle the situation. At that time, she wasn't close to anyone at Canby Hall, so she kept her feelings about M.B. to herself and chalked her up as a thoughtless snob.

It was months before Shelley ever mentioned Mary Beth, and then only because Dana brought her up in conversation. Dana was on the committee for Song Night, which took place soon after the winter break. Song Night consisted of an evening of songs sung by the students — old, new, and original — everything from love ballads to the Beatles to rock and New Wave. Dana, who was generally outgoing and friendly, stood next to Mary Beth in the soprano section of the Canby Hall Choir. Dana was looking for participants for Song Night and approached everyone who had a passable voice. Mary Beth had a strong rich tone, but Dana hesitated to ask her to sing.

Mary Beth was an enigma to Dana, as well as to anyone else who had dealings with her. Dana, after several unsuccessful attempts to be friendly, finally gave up. She couldn't figure her out. Mary Beth, with her ivory complexion, soft wavy hair, and deep brown eyes, was exceptionally pretty. She had a slim, five-foot-five figure and dressed well, but seemed intent on blending with her environment so that no one would notice her. She rarely smiled, never talked with anyone between classes or during rehearsal breaks, and might as well have been wrapped in a cocoon to protect her from human contact.

Mary Beth sang in chorus as an alternative to taking a music appreciation course and played as a substitute on the tennis team in order to fulfill her phys-ed requirements. She was good at everything and was academically successful, making the tenth grade 'honors' list after the first semester. It was odd that she didn't seem to enjoy anything — just went through the motions, did what was required but, because of her intelligence, did well.

Dana's run-in with Mary Beth took place less than a week before the Christmas holidays were to begin, and the Song Night committee was beginning to feel the crunch of lining up people to perform. Partly as a desperate measure, but also because she had literally touched shoulders with Mary Beth at least once a week and knew she had a good voice, Dana decided to ask her if she'd be interested.

The choir had just finished rehearsing the Hallelujah chorus of the *Messiah*, which was to be featured at the winter concert the following Sunday. Mr. Brewster, the skinny, nervous conductor who rarely complimented anyone, had just praised the singers for making such good music in such a short amount of time. Dana, like everyone else, was high on his flattery as well as the excitement generated by the music and decided it was the perfect time to approach Mary Beth.

Mr. Brewster announced a fifteen-minute break before working on the Christmas carols that would round out the program. There was a general feeling of excitement in the air, and everyone was buzzing together. Only Mary Beth sat by herself, on the aisle in the middle of the auditorium away from the crowd, inconspicuous as always. Her head was bent over her music, as though she were studying the notes, when Dana approached her.

"Hi," Dana began brightly. "Good rehearsal, right?" Dana seated herself on the arm of the chair across the aisle.

"Not bad," Mary Beth answered.

"I always get tingles during those last measures, no matter how many times I hear the *Messiah.*"

"I guess that's true for a lot of people, otherwise it wouldn't be performed all the time."

Dana felt the conversation was going nowhere, so she decided to plunge right in with her original purpose. "You've got a really good voice, you know, Mary Beth, and I wondered if you'd be interested in doing something for Song Night. You could sing anything you want."

"Not interested," Mary Beth remarked.

"It's a lot of fun," Dana persisted. "The best amateur night in town, and standing room only. Brings out all the guys from Oakley Prep as well as the public school."

"Thanks, but no thanks."

"But this could make you a star!" Dana thought maybe she could tease Mary Beth into action.

"That's the last thing I want to be," Mary Beth said evenly. "End of discussion."

"I guess you mean it," Dana decided, and slowly moved away, feeling put down and angry.

That night when she got back to her room at Baker House — one of the three dorms on the beautifully landscaped campus — she described her encounter with Mary Beth to her roommates. Then, for the first time, Shelley told her laundry-room story.

"I guess she's just unreal," Dana surmised.

"It's hard to understand why," Faith said thoughtfully. "Maybe she's got reasons."

"Maybe," Shelley conceded, as she carefully tidied up her desk. "But who has time to figure out what they are? Not me, for sure."

"For sure," Dana echoed, and after that the subject was closed.

Therefore, it came as a complete surprise that Faith would consider approaching Mary Beth for the *Clarion* story. Almost five

months had passed since they had discussed
her, but the mere mention of her name triggered a strong negative reaction from Dana
and Shelley.

"There must be a zillion kids better qualified." Shelley, who was generally good-
natured and was not the kind to bear a
grudge, couldn't quite forgive M.B. for treat-
ing her in such an offhand manner at a time
when Shelley was so vulnerable.

"Not really," Faith said. "Also, maybe she
deserves another chance — a little attention."
Faith couldn't help having sympathetic feelings for an outsider, any outsider, especially
at Canby Hall. She was savvy about herself,
as well as others, but she knew what it was
like to feel out of things and different. Even
though Faith was a very good student, and
generally secure about herself, and Dana,
the authority on appearance, described her
as a "stunner," it had taken her quite awhile
to feel accepted at Canby Hall. She believed
her difficulties were a result of her being one
of the very few black students.

In the public school in Washington, D.C.,
Faith had had a number of white friends, but
those friendships had evolved over the years.
At Canby Hall, she'd been thrust into an
almost all-white environment, and her two
roommates were white, and in the beginning
Faith had to cope with both those prejudices
she imagined and those that were real.

Shelley, whose experience was limited to small-town life in Pine Bluff, Iowa, where the Fourth of July church picnic was the main social event of the year, was in awe of Faith. Faith's Afro hairdo and long, leggy body, along with her confidence and sharp wit, was too much for Shelley. Shelley's way of coping with such an exotic girl, who like herself was fifteen years old but seemed light years ahead of her in experience, was avoidance. Understandably, Faith thought she was prejudiced. And the more Shelley learned about Faith's background — her widowed mother was a highly respected social worker and politically active, her father was a policeman who was killed on duty in an attempted bank robbery — the more alien Faith seemed.

Shelley, whose only ambition in life at that time was to be a homemaker and mother, felt more at ease when she learned that Faith, too, wanted to marry, as well as be a photojournalist. That was the first indication to Shelley that maybe they weren't worlds apart.

In Pine Bluff, the friends of Shelley's mother didn't work outside of their home except to help out in their husband's business or in times of economic necessity. Shelley's defensiveness about her mother's homemaker role was intensified when she learned that Faith's mother was a professional and Dana's mother, who was divorced and had always been a working mother, had a high-powered job as a buyer in a department store in New York City. Shelley felt unworldly compared to her big-city roommates, but was somewhat relieved to discover that Dana and Faith, like more than half of the Canby Hall students including herself, had partial scholarships.

Gradually, the lines of difference between the roommates faded. They were still three distinct personalities, but their differences, instead of separating them, made them more interested in each other. They began to respect rather than feel threatened by their dissimilar backgrounds, and they shared a sense of humor that saw them through some tight spots. Now they could kid one another about elements of their lives that previously were unmentionable. That's why, when Faith suggested that Mary Beth should be given another chance, Shelley remarked, "Faith, your social worker genes are showing."

"Maybe," Faith said, thoughtfully, "but she does live in the heart of Boston, and I've seen her taking a lot of pictures lately. Always of things, not people, which leads me to believe she'd be perfect for photographing houses."

"You may be right," Dana said with her usual optimism.

"I guess you can't hurt a house's feelings," Shelley remarked.

"Especially if no one's living in it," Faith added. Faith's humor often bordered on the sarcastic, which was a protective covering for her genuine feelings of sensitivity toward others.

"You have a back-up candidate, don't you?" Dana asked:

"Judy Barnes is just as well qualified. But she's a regular contributor and Mr. Bowker, who is the *Clarion* faculty advisor, keeps talking about 'involving' other students in extra-curricular activities. He's a nut on the subject, but he's got a point. That's another reason I'll try for Mary Beth."

"When are you going to ask her?" Dana inquired. She had wrapped her head and face with the shawl so that only her eyes were exposed.

"First thing tomorrow. We have English together, and I'll catch her before class begins."

"*Bonne chance!*" Dana spoke in her best French accent.

"*Quel dommage!*" Shelley corrected her.

After almost failing French Shelley was doing so well she could now drop phrases such as "what a pity," into the conversation.

"Whatever you say, I'm going to try," Faith asserted.

Faith was concerned about whether she was doing the right thing in approaching Mary Beth, but her anxiety didn't rub off on her roommates. Shelley, obviously elated with having finished the sleeve, pulled it on her head like a dunce cap. Then she leapt up from the floor and began skipping in circles around the veiled Dana, who stopped admiring herself in the mirror and held herself like a statue. It was hard for Faith to remain serious as she watched their antics. As often happened when the three of them were together for any length of time, they found themselves dissolved in laughter.

"How would I ever get along without you two idiots?" Faith asked.

No one bothered to answer that question because they all felt the same way.

CHAPTER
TWO

The next morning Faith made a point of arriving at English class before the first bell rang. She hoped to catch Mary Beth on her way in. Mr. Washburn, the sarcastic teacher who didn't hesitate to embarrass his students, was a softie under his hard exterior. He loved teaching even though he behaved like a tyrant on occasion.

Faith waited outside in the corridor and then a few minutes before the second bell sounded she saw Mary Beth, predictably alone, walking down the hall. Faith approached her when she was still a few yards away from the doorway. "Wanted to ask you something, Mary Beth."

Mary Beth stiffened and paled. "What?" she asked, her eyes widening in alarm. She reminded Faith of a startled rabbit.

"I've noticed you taking a lot of pictures

lately, and I thought you might like to photo-graph a story for the *Clarion*." Faith kept her voice as soft as possible in order not to frighten her. "It's our last issue of the year, you know, and we want to do a feature on historic homes of Boston. There are half a dozen that —"

"I don't want to," Mary Beth interrupted.

"You're the perfect person. You obviously like taking pictures, and you're familiar with the area. You're a natural for —"

"No!" Mary Beth cried.

"But you might enjoy it. You'll get a credit and —"

"*Forget it*, will you?" With that, she rushed off, leaving Faith totally bewildered.

Faith went into the classroom and slid into her seat in the back of the room. She was grateful that Washburn was almost ten min-utes late, which gave her a chance to recover from Mary Beth's bizarre reaction. Faith couldn't understand why she was such a loner. She couldn't dismiss Mary Beth's anti-social behavior as easily as her roommates. Maybe, as Shelley would say, her social worker genes were showing, but Faith sensed something very deep was bothering Mary Beth. She behaved like someone who had a terrible secret. Why else would she have turned ashen when Faith had said to her in a friendly manner that she wanted to ask her something? And why had she been so definite about not taking on an assignment as innocent and less fraught with danger as taking pictures of homes?

Faith puzzled over these questions until Washburn burst into the room and immediately began quizzing the students on their vocabulary homework. His technique was to shoot off at machine-gun pace the words that should have been memorized. After stating the word, he picked out a student and gave her exactly two seconds to come up with the correct definition. If the answer was right, he flashed a brief but brilliant smile and put a check beside the girl's name on his class list, and if the answer was wrong, he scowled.

At the beginning of the semester, he promised that everyone who earned enough checks — he never stated the number required — would be invited to a party at his house, one of the faculty houses surrounded by trees. The pastry party was a tradition, and no one taking English with Mr. Washburn had ever been excluded, no matter how far behind in her assignments. In that sense, it was all a game that no one could lose, but it had the desired effect because no one enjoyed looking like a dumbbell in front of the class and being frowned at by the teacher. Only Millie Ogden, the class joke nicknamed Willie Nillie Millie by some of the less-than-kind tenth graders, never was prepared.

Millie was a small wispy girl from Cleve-

land who no one paid much attention to or
thought about — except when she goofed.
Millie was the classic example of someone
who was picked last for the teams on which
the lineups weren't arranged by Ms. Gorman
of the phys ed department. Team sports com-
petition was always among the three dorms
— Baker, Charles, and Addison. In volleyball
matches, Millie instinctively backed away
from the ball, and the competing team was
guaranteed a sure point if the ball was aimed
at her. In field hockey, she was paralyzed
with fear. And in the spring when softball
was the most popular team sport, Millie was
put in left field where it was obvious she
hoped the ball never reached her. She was
such a hopeless drawback that the opponents
generously avoided taking advantage of her.

As usual Millie failed to define the words
that Washburn asked her, but she didn't
seem the least upset, even though the class
laughed. Millie was seemingly immune to
people's opinions and since she was so mild,
she was quickly overlooked.

As Mr. Washburn continued his barrage of
questions, Faith's mind wandered back to
Mary Beth. Faith had totally shed her earlier
feelings of isolation, and with each successive
week of school had become more secure,
more involved with outside activities, and
more able to help girls who had never quite
recovered from the homesickness that was a

common condition of every new Canby Hall student. Each girl had her own way of coping and most of them succeeded, but Mary Beth was an exception. As time went by she became more frozen in her position. Faith couldn't imagine being anywhere without someone to talk to.

How awful, Faith thought. Faith decided that as soon as English was over, she'd ask Mary Beth to meet her at the Tutti-Frutti, which was the afternoon hangout in the village of Greenleaf. The twenty-six varieties of ice cream made it a decision-making exercise as well as a place to go. It occurred to Faith that in all the times she'd gone into the village, either to buy an ice-cream cone, check out the candy store, or pig out at the pizza place, she'd never seen Mary Beth.

There were only two months left of school and Faith, who had happily resolved her early problems, shuddered to think what it would be like to have been friendless the entire year. Mary Beth's isolation was exaggerated by the fact that she was one of the few first-year students who had opted for a single room. That meant that, except for choir and tennis and some other required group activities, she was alone, usually holed up in her room. Her room, 417 in Baker, was located at the far end of the hall, and her dormmates seldom passed by.

Washburn wrote the next day's homework

assignment on the blackboard, and Faith
promptly copied it down in her notebook.
Then she dumped her pads and pencils in her
canvas bag so that she would be ready to
leave as soon as class was dismissed. When
the bell rang, Faith hurried out and went up
to Mary Beth. As casually as possible, she
said, "How about meeting me in the village
for an ice-cream cone after school?"

Mary Beth stopped cold and stared at
Faith. For a brief second, a smile flickered on
her face, and Faith thought she had broken
through. But then she replied, without hesitation, "No thanks."

"Why not, Mary Beth? It's a gorgeous day
— perfect for ice cream."

"I just can't," she answered, and then in
order to ward off any further questions she
added, "I have to go now or I'll be late for
History."

Faith's next class was math, so they had
to go in opposite directions. That meant
Faith couldn't have continued the conversation even if Mary Beth hadn't cut her short.
The warning bell rang and they separated
without another word.

Faith felt rejected, annoyed, and angry.
She had extended herself on two levels, work
and friendship, and neither had worked. She
wasn't as convinced as her roommates that
Mary Beth was a super snob, but she knew it
was useless to try to reach her. In spite of

the nagging concern she still felt, Faith told
herself it was Mary Beth's life, not hers, and
there wasn't much else she could do. She
settled down in her math class and tried to
focus on Mr. Kogan, the brilliant new teacher
who tried to disguise his youth with a Van-
dyke beard.

Faith didn't get a chance to talk to Shelley
and Dana until she got back to their room
after five o'clock. Each girl had her own
extracurricular activity. Dana was in a special madrigal group that was rehearsing regu-
larly for graduation day ceremonies. Shelley
had a big part in a new play, which excited
her. She had recently decided to be an actress, and she was serious about it and
worked hard. Faith had been asked by Patrice Allardyce, the aloof but elegant headmistress, to show some prospective students
around the campus after her last class. This
was the first time the girls had been alone
together all day.

Shelley was sitting on the edge of her bed
where she had spread out a collection of
earrings she had acquired over the past few
months. Faith and Dana frequently teased
her about her odd purchases of junk jewelry,
but she was addicted. Whenever she was let
loose in Greenleaf, she zeroed in on the
local jewelry store and invariably bought
whatever sale item struck her fancy.

"Aren't these something?" Shelley asked Dana, just as Faith walked in. Shelley was holding up a pair of purple feather earrings.

Dana looked up from her desk, where she was writing a letter to her mother thanking her for the shawl, and silently appraised the dangling objects.

"You want the truth?" Dana didn't want to hurt Shelley's feelings, but for the past six months she'd been trying to improve her cornfield cutesy style.

"I guess you don't like them," Shelley sighed, but started to put them on anyways. Then she turned to Faith, who had just flopped down on her bed. "What do you think, Faith? You've got good taste."

"They're a beautiful color," Faith said tactfully.

"I know what that means," Shelley said, "but I'm going to wear them anyways."

"Feather earrings are *out*. They would have been fine a year or two ago," Dana explained.

"I'm wrong again," Shelley grumbled good-naturedly.

"You weren't wrong about Mary Beth, though," Faith said. "When I asked her about taking pictures, you would have thought I'd suggested she jump naked into the wishing pond in front of the entire school."

"She refused, I guess," Dana said.

"She ran away from me."

"Did you ask Judy Barnes?" Dana reminded Faith.

"I just caught her on the way over here, and she can't wait."

"It's funny," Dana remarked thoughtfully, "we've each had a similar experience with Mary Beth. She just doesn't want to be friendly. Why?"

"It proves she's off the wall," Shelley said. "If she can't bring herself to talk to three such fascinating women as ourselves, there must be something basically wrong."

"That's what I think, but what else can we do?" Dana said.

"Nothing," Shelley answered.

And Faith had to agree.

Dana wondered what Bret would think about Mary Beth. Bret Harper was Dana's boyfriend, who went to nearby Oakley Prep. He had been the sheik of the campus, dating one girl after another, until he met Dana. He was totally crazy about her and didn't look at another girl now — hardly. In spite of his preppy background, amazing good looks, and casual sense of humor, he had sensitivity and insight into people. Dana thought, *I'll talk to Bret about this when I see him.*

Dana felt a great surge of love for Bret, when she remembered how he had unquestioningly helped her and Faith hunt for Shelley after she had been kidnapped. For Danā it had been further proof of how special Bret was.

He'd also been so helpful when she'd had to tell her father she was not going to go to live with him and his new wife in Hawaii for a year. It hadn't been easy, but Bret had been wonderful, encouraging her to make her own decision and stick with it.

Dana went back to her letter and let Shelley wear whatever earrings she wanted.

CHAPTER THREE

Faith awakened early the next morning, almost fifteen minutes before the seven o'clock alarm went off. The sun was already filtering through the batik curtains that Shelley had made especially for 407. Faith quietly pulled herself out of bed, not wanting to disturb Shelley and Dana, and glanced out the window that overlooked the park. The park landscaped with birch trees and the wishing pool stocked with golden carp were fresh and dewey and glistening with the morning sun.

Faith took a deep breath and had an almost overwhelming sense of well-being. Things were going so well, she was more grateful than ever for the opportunity to attend Canby Hall.

She knew it wasn't financially easy for her mother to send her to private school, even with a scholarship. Her sister, Sarah, was attending Georgetown University, where the tuition was also steep. Her kid brother, Richard, was still in junior high. Sarah, although three years older than Faith, was a good friend to her as well as a role model. Faith was thrilled that she had been able to live up to her mother's expectations as well as the standards that Sarah had set. She couldn't wait to write home about being tapped by the headmistress to represent the school to girls who were applying for admission. Dana and Shelley agreed that any sign of favorable recognition from the elegant and mysterious Ms. Allardyce was a real plum, and they joked about the glory that had been bestowed on Faith.

As soon as the alarm rang, Faith pulled herself away from the window and padded down the hall to the bathroom. This was the one room in the dorm that had an institutional atmosphere. There were stalls, showers, and a bank of sinks long enough to accommodate five girls at one time, but Faith relished the few minutes of privacy that getting up early provided. She luxuriated in a hot shower and shampooed her hair before the girls on her floor began floating in.

By the time she got back to her room, Shelley and Dana were just getting up.

"It's another fantastic day, guys. It's Friday and there are no extracurricular activities scheduled, so let's take advantage of it."

"What do you have in mind?" Dana rubbed her eyes sleepily.

"We should go into the village after our last class. I've got to find a birthday present for my sister. She's into country music so I think I'll send her a record. That's about all I can afford."

"I'd love to go to town. I haven't been in Jim's Gems for over a week. He's probably worried about me." Shelley was quite serious.

"I think it makes a lot of sense that you pay him a visit." Dana tried not to laugh at Shelley's naivete.

Dana had noticed that since Shelley had gone through the terrifying experience of being kidnapped earlier that year, she seemed to be buying more junk than ever. As if she was giving herself silly presents just for the joy of being alive.

"Absolutely. Otherwise he may be rounding up some German shepherds to put on your trail." Faith was good-humoredly sarcastic.

"Oh, you two . . ." Shelley grinned.

"Actually," Dana said, "I'd like to check out the Second Time Round Shoppe for an antique blouse. Not that I can afford it, but maybe Prudence will let me buy one on the installment plan. Ever since she learned my mother was a buyer for a New York department store, she's been extra nice."

"Plus the fact that you're a terrific model for her clothes," Faith observed.

"Yeah, maybe she should pay *you* for wearing them," Shelley offered.

"That's a good idea," Dana said. "I'll split whatever I make with you — my two closest friends."

Prudence was the uptight owner of the used clothes store and very rigid about rules. Browsing was okay, but no ice cream or candy bars, and she'd been known to ask girls to wash their hands before trying on clothes.

"Let's go our separate ways and meet at the Tutti-Frutti at four o'clock," Faith suggested.

"Neat," Shelley said. "That'll give me plenty of time to make a selection." She dragged herself out of bed and headed for the door. "Coming, Dana?"

"Not till I finish my daily dozen," she mumbled as she proceeded to do some sit-ups. "Save me a sink."

It was arranged that Faith sign out the three of them on the sheet that was posted on the front of their door and then meet them at the gatehouse. On the way, Shelley went into minute detail about the frog she had to dissect in biology.

"I couldn't believe I was doing it. That adorable little frog, and I was playing doctor."

"It's all in the interest of science," Dana consoled her.

"I don't know. I don't think the world of biology will benefit from my learning the location of a frog's heart."

"But it might lead someone to make a great scientific discovery," Faith argued.

"It won't be me. The whole thing grossed me out, but at least I didn't have to leave the room to barf the way Millie did."

"You're kidding," Dana exclaimed.

"Nope. She made this mad scramble out the door, muttering something about getting sick, and came back a few minutes later looking the same pale green as the frog."

"What'd she say?" Dana asked. "She must have died of embarrassment."

"Didn't seem to. In fact, Mr. Farber asked her if she didn't want to be excused for the rest of the lab period, but she muttered something about feeling okay and she just had to get used to the smell of formaldehyde."

"She actually stuck it out?" Dana was surprised. "That is one strange girl. She doesn't seem to mind that people think she can't do anything right."

"She got through the class fine and the whole thing was forgotten. I thought that maybe I should fake being sick — faint or something dramatic like that — but I didn't think of it in time."

"I can see the headline now in the Pine Bluff *Gazette*," Faith teased: "LOCAL GIRL INCAPACITATED BY EASTERN FROG."

The three of them cracked up at the absurdity, and by the time they stopped giggling, were already in Greenleaf.

"I think we better split now. We've all got things to do," Dana advised.

"I agree. We'll meet at four at the Tutti-Frutti as planned." Faith was practical, as always.

"That only gives me an hour," Shelley complained.

"You don't have to spend all your money in one day," Dana said.

"It's not that. I just need time to look, and Jim's will take a while, and I may not get back here till next week . . ." Then she realized that Dana and Faith were looking at her indulgently and she was sounding like a baby, so she promptly stopped whining and yelled, "See ya."

Less than fifty feet away was the record store, the Music Box, and Faith waved to Dana as she disappeared inside. The records were precisely displayed according to category, and she immediately headed for the country music bin. Faith knew she would be there all day if she debated about which one Sarah would like best, so she picked out a Duane Allen and the Oakridge Boys album, and took it to the rumpled-looking man behind the counter.

"Nice to see somebody who's able to make up her mind around here. Usually takes 'em hours." His voice was dour, but there was a twinkle in his eye.

"It's a birthday present for my sister, and she likes anything that's country."

"Smart girl," he growled, taking the bill Faith had handed him and opening the cash register. "Would you like me to wrap it for you?"

"That would be great. I can mail it to her from school."

"Canby Hall girl, I bet." He returned the change and then turned away to pull out a sheaf of wrapping paper that was on the shelf behind him.

Faith felt a small glow at being identified as a Canby girl. It gave her a strong sense of identity, of a connection with all Canby Hall girls. "That's right, Mr. Jones," she replied. There was a name plate, LAWRENCE JONES, OWNER, on the counter.

"Can always tell," he bragged, and presented her with the record that he had wrapped in embossed silver paper and tied with a bright red cord.

"That's beautiful. Thank you so much," Faith said, and started to leave.

She was halfway out the door when she heard him grumbling, "Wish all my customers were like her."

Faith strolled up the street to the Tutti-Frutti, smiling all the way. She knew she'd be at least a half-hour ahead of Shelley and

Dana, but the idea of sitting on one of the benches under the awning of the store and watching the world go by was very appealing.

There were two lines of people leaning against the glass counter where the ice cream was displayed in large tubs. Mothers with babies, older couples, kids — a whole cross-section of Greenleaf was waiting to be served by the two girls in the green-and-white-striped shirts who worked behind the counter. Faith didn't mind the wait because it gave her time to decide on what flavor she should choose. When it was her turn, she asked for a double cone of maple walnut and pistachio mint. The scooper girl handed her the cone along with a check, and then she had to stand in another line near the exit in order to pay. She was digging in her canvas tote bag for the correct amount of change when she felt a cold slap on her shoulder.

"Oh, no," a deep voice groaned behind her.

"I didn't mean it," a little girl squeaked. "My dumb brother pushed me, and I bumped into you and it's all his fault . . ."

Faith looked at her shoulder and saw that a glob of strawberry ice cream was on her shoulder and trickling down her arm. She was wearing a short-sleeved mauve T-shirt and, for an insane instant, thought how perfectly the colors blended.

"It's okay, kid. You didn't do it on purpose,"

the person behind her, whose cone was now on her shoulder, said.

Faith turned around, annoyed. She was all set to say, "It's not okay for me," but the words stuck in her throat when she saw who was responsible. He looked about seventeen, was almost a head taller than Faith, black, handsome, with the deepest brown eyes she'd ever seen. When he smiled at her apologetically, Faith thought she might melt more quickly than the ice cream.

"I'm really sorry," he said.

The two of them stared at each other for at least thirty seconds. Then some man behind them yelled, "I haven't got all day. Let's move it!"

Faith hadn't realized that she was now at the head of the line and fumbled in her canvas bag for some money.

"The least I can do is pay for your cone," the boy volunteered.

"Oh no, that's all right," Faith said firmly.

"I insist," he said authoritatively, took the check from her, and paid the cashier for both their cones. Then he grabbed a bunch of paper napkins from the counter and guided Faith to a booth in the back of the ice cream parlor.

Faith collected herself as he leaned across the table and dabbed at her shoulder with the napkins and then wiped away the ice cream from her arm. Her arm tingled — and not just from the ice cream.

"Your cone is ruined," she said idiotically, after he'd mopped up.

"Not enough to need a replacement. Besides, now it's got a special shoulder flavor," he assured her.

"That's the first time anyone's given me a real cold shoulder." She laughed easily.

"I'm glad you've got a sense of humor." He beamed a toothpaste smile at her.

He is cute, Faith thought, *but I don't even know his name.*

"We don't know each other's names," he remarked, and Faith was sure he had mind-reading talents as well as good looks.

"I'm Faith Thompson, a sophomore at Canby Hall."

"And I'm Johnny Bates, a junior at Greenleaf High."

"Hi."

"Hi."

After they got through the preliminaries, Faith glanced at her watch. "It's after four, and I'm meeting my roommates. They're probably out front so I really have to go."

"It was great bumping into you," Johnny said. "I don't get away in the afternoon much these days because I've been helping my father out at his gas station. Things were slow so he told me to take a break, but I should be getting back."

"Do you work for him all year round?"

"Only in an emergency. My folks want me to concentrate on school so that I can get a scholarship to college. I'm at the station now because my father's assistant wrenched his back."

"That must be a guy's dream — to mess around with cars. I bet you want to be a mechanical engineer."

"No way," Johnny was adamant. "I want to be a detective."

"A detective?" Faith's eyes suddenly clouded, and she felt a knot in her stomach.

"Did I say something wrong?" Johnny couldn't figure out why she looked so startled.

"Yes . . . no . . . I mean it's nothing personal — only it is. That is . . ." She was floundering again and was saved by Dana and Shelley, who were striding into the back room, licking their ice cream cones.

"There you are!" Shelley called. "I told Dana you'd probably be back here saving us a booth." She was about to slide in next to Faith.

"I was just going to look for you," Faith said.

"We can meet you outside," Dana suggested tactfully. "Shel wanted me to look at something at Jim's. She can't make up her mind about which bangle bracelets to buy."

"Oh, yeah." Shelley picked up the hint that

maybe they should leave Faith alone with this really cute guy.

"These are my roommates, Dana Morrison and Shelley Hyde. This is Johnny Bates." Faith introduced everyone.

They exchanged hi's, and Johnny asked them to sit down.

"Thanks, but we don't have much time before we have to get back," Dana explained. Then she turned to Faith. "We'll wait for you at Jim's."

As subtly as possible, she nudged Shelley off before Shelley could interfere with whatever was going on between Faith and Johnny.

"I hope I can see you again — like maybe tomorrow if I don't have to work," Johnny said as soon as the others had left.

"Well, I don't know. I . . . maybe." Faith was totally confused because before he'd mentioned his ambition to be a detective, she would have certainly wanted to see him again.

"Look, Faith, I don't want to press you. And I have to admit that this was a weird way to meet. But . . ."

"It's not the way we met," Faith said. "It's something else."

"You're very mysterious, but if you decide you want to see me, here's my number."

He took a pencil out of the pocket of his shirt, wrote down his telephone number on a napkin, and handed it to her.

She slipped the napkin into her tote bag and slid out of the booth.

"Thanks for the cone," she said as he stood up and started to lead the way to the door.

When they were outside, Johnny, before backing away and flashing that dazzling smile, said, "If nothing else, I had a great coffee break."

"Me, too," she agreed, before she realized how silly that was. It wasn't a coffee break for her, but Johnny had already gone off before she could explain. Anyhow, she didn't want to encourage him, did she? Not unless she wanted to see him again. And she wasn't sure about that, not if his ambition in life was to be a cop.

She remembered the day her father had died. The pain and disbelief she had felt. It didn't matter to her that he had died a hero, trying to stop a bank robbery. He was dead, and she didn't want to get involved ever again with anyone who was a policeman. No matter how nice he seemed.

She was still standing there, watching Johnny gracefully walk off into the distance, when Shelley came charging up to her.

"Dana can't make up her mind either about which bangles I should get — the mother-of-pearl or the ones that look like jade. It's up to you, Faith. You never have trouble making up your mind."

"Sure," Faith complied, and followed Shel-

ley to the jewelry store thinking how true
that was — she didn't have trouble making
up her mind — until less than an hour ago
when she met Johnny.

That night Dana had a special date with
Bret. Special because they were going to be
alone, something they agreed didn't happen
nearly often enough. Usually they went out
with at least one other couple, meeting a
bunch of kids at the movies or the Pizza
Palace in Greenleaf. But Bret was going to
pick her up in a half-hour and drive to a
seafood restaurant on the shore where there
were outdoor tables and dancing under the
stars.

She hummed to herself as she slipped into
a dark red linen shift and dark red sandals.
She tossed her shawl over her shoulders,
feeling on top of the world. *I'm lucky, lucky,
lucky* she thought as she flew down the stairs
to meet Bret.

The evening started off perfectly, with
Bret complimenting her. "You look smashing," he said as they walked toward his car.

"Then we must be a smashing couple,"
Dana laughed, which was her way of returning the compliment.

Bret was, without question, the best-
looking boy Dana had ever known. Tall, dark,
and handsome was a cliché, but also an

accurate description. But best of all, he was bright, sensitive, and generous.

Their date was even better than Dana anticipated. As she danced in Bret's arms, she thought she'd never been happier. She thought there must be a glow around them, because people smiled admiringly when they walked into the restaurant and when they got up to dance.

She floated through the evening, and when she got back to the dorm, she and Faith and Shelley went over their day.

CHAPTER FOUR

Shelley talked on about the mother-of-pearl bangles being a wiser choice since they would go with everything and how she appreciated Dana and Faith's contribution to the decision-making process.

"I don't know how I'll ever be able to buy anything without consulting you two."

"You've come a long way, baby," Dana reminded her. "When you first got here you thought the more colors you could wear at one time the better."

"I know, I know. Now look at what I wear — beige cords and a pale yellow shirt that matches my hair. I look like a mouse!"

"Not you," Dana objected. "It's known as monochromatic in the fashion world."

"Monochromatic, it sounds like a disease," Shelley exclaimed.

"Don't tell that to the designers. They'll think you're out to ruin them."

The two of them talked back and forth. But Faith was deep in her own thoughts and hadn't participated in any of the banter. It wasn't like Faith to be so quiet, and Dana was suddenly sensitive to the fact that she hadn't said a word.

"That Johnny is certainly a cute guy!" Dana said.

"You two looked perfect together," Shelley added.

"We did?" Faith was pleased with the idea of being thought of as part of a couple for the first time in her life.

"You're going to see him again, aren't you?" Shelley went on.

"I don't know. I'd like to, but . . ."

"Do you have his number?" Dana asked.

"Yes, but it doesn't mean I have to use it."

"Why not. He wouldn't have given it to you if he didn't want you to call." Dana waited for Faith to say something.

"There are a lot of problems."

"Already? That's impossible . . . you hardly know each other. In my vast experience, you should give it a chance —" Shelley said.

"Shel," Dana interrupted, "maybe we should change the subject. You know, sometimes we come on like gangbusters — bang, bang, bang."

"That's just the problem," Faith murmured. "He wants to be a cop." These were her two best friends, and there was no point in keeping her feelings a secret.

"After the way my father died, I can't imagine going out with someone who is going to be a policeman. It really upsets me. But maybe, like you said, I should give it a chance. He left it up to me whether I should call or not. What do you think, Dana?"

"Well, you remember my experience with Bret. If you hadn't made me call him at one point last semester I might never have spoken to him again. Remember when he took that Polly Talbot to the Harvest Holiday dance?"

"I remember and it certainly worked out okay for you," Shelley said.

"You have nothing to lose. It's not a life-time commitment." Shelley could not resist encouraging Faith, and considered herself an authority on men. After all, she had two older brothers at Iowa State who treated her like a princess even though they called her Slugger. She also had Paul, whom she had grown up with and whom, when she came to Canby Hall, she had thought she would surely marry. Then, when she had tried out for a school play she had met Tom Stevenson, a town boy who went to Greenleaf High and had a part in the play. Her strong attraction to him had confused her. If she was in love

with Paul, how could she love Tom, too? She
had finally decided that she didn't have to
decide *anything* at this point in her life.

"Thanks for all your advice," Faith said.
"I'll think about it tonight, and tomorrow
I'll wake up with the answer . . . I hope."

"Forgive me for saying this, Faith," Shelley
chuckled, "but I'm glad for once it's you who's
having love problems."

"Who said anything about love?" Faith
asked. "I hardly know him."

"All the more reason you should see him
again," Shelley persisted.

"She's right, you know," Dana added.

"Maybe . . . maybe . . ." Faith mused
dreamily, "and maybe he'll think about another career."

Faith fell asleep thinking of Johnny, weighing the pros and cons of calling him. The
minute she awakened the next morning, she
knew she had to see Johnny again.

On Saturdays, the whole dorm slept late.
Faith leapt out of bed, grabbed Johnny's
number and some change from her bag, and
flew down the stairs to the main floor where
there was a phone booth. She was so out of
breath that she collapsed on a bench in the
reception room, thinking how eerie it was to
be sitting barefoot and in pajamas in this
formal atmosphere. She was unexpectedly

nervous about making the call — what should she say, might he put her off, was he just being polite, why hadn't she insisted that he call her. All these questions plagued her, and she muttered to herself, "Might as well get it over with."

She was heading for the phone booth when the grandfather clock, one of the valuable antiques that belonged to the original Canby estate, caught Faith's attention. It had begun its distinctive deep chime and Faith idly counted — one, two, three, four, five, six, seven, eight. A ridiculous hour for any Canby Hall girl to be up on a Saturday, but Faith figured that the Bates family would be early risers if Mr. Bates ran a gas station.

Faith was in the corridor, rehearsing her opening line in her head — *Hi, Johnny, it's me, Faith, the girl you met at the Tutti-Frutti*. Or maybe more laid-back — *Sorry to be calling so early, but I may not get another chance all day*. No, she thought, that sounded like a lie, and it was. Just do it, she told herself, looking down at Johnny's number as she walked toward the phone. The next thing she knew, someone coming out of the phone booth crashed into her. She was frightened out of her skin but was relieved to see it was Mary Beth and not a stranger. Mary Beth was dressed in a pleated gray skirt and a pale blue blouse. Her usual pale complexion was flushed, and she seemed to panic when she saw that she had collided with Faith.

"I thought I was the only one who got up before breakfast." Faith wanted to put her at ease. "What are you doing here so early?"

"Had to make a call," she whispered, and glanced around as though she were afraid of being overheard.

"Me, too," Faith said. She hadn't forgotten how annoyed she'd been with Mary Beth, but it was hard to stay angry at a wounded bird.

"I have to go now." Mary Beth, still flustered, brushed by Faith and sped up the stairs.

Faith shrugged her shoulders in disbelief, but she had other things to think about. Before she could chicken out and change her mind, she went into the phone booth and dialed Johnny's number. She hoped he would answer so that she didn't have to cope with his mother or father. It was awfully early and they would naturally be curious why a strange girl was calling their son at this hour.

The phone rang once, twice, three times and with each successive ring, Faith became less certain that she was doing the right thing. Then someone picked up, and Faith held her breath until a deep, rich voice that she knew, said hello.

"It's me, Faith Thompson, I didn't know if it was too early to call but because of your father's gas station and you having to work maybe, I wanted to catch you because I know —"

"Faith," Johnny interrupted, smoothly. "You called, and I'm glad."

"You are?" Faith knew she'd been rattling on like a nerd, but he sounded so genuinely pleased to hear from her that she regained her composure.

"As a matter of fact, if you hadn't, I would have. I was going to call you this afternoon for sure."

"I hope I didn't wake up anybody in your house." Faith was totally in control of herself again and could talk sensibly.

"My father's already gone to work, and as you can tell, I didn't have to go with him. His assistant's okay now."

"What about your mother?"

"She's always up at the crack of dawn, even on weekends that she doesn't work at the hospital. I guess I inherited that from her . . . I can never sleep late. When can I see you?"

"Whenever," Faith replied.

"It looks like another wonderful day. Maybe we could have a picnic."

"Terrific. There's this really neat spot near the skating pond that was meant for picnics.

Trees, aquamarine water, wild flowers — it looks like a setting for a Renoir painting."

"Do you think peanut butter sandwiches would ruin the scene? I could make some at home and pick up some Tabs on the way over," Johnny said.

"I don't think Renoir would mind. My contribution will be pretzels and mustard."

"Pretzels and mustard! I never heard of such a combination."

"You don't know what you're missing, Johnny."

Faith quickly asked what time she should be ready.

"Twelve okay? I'm working on a term paper for my sociology class, and I want to go to the public library to check out some facts."

"Twelve is fine. Meet me in front of Baker House, which is the center dorm."

"See ya, Faith. And thanks for calling."

"Later," Faith said, and slowly hung up the receiver.

Then she floated upstairs and into her room where Dana and Shelley were still sound asleep. It was good not to have to talk to anyone, and she snuggled under the covers, daydreaming about Johnny. He'd been so friendly and honest. He wasn't interested in playing games, or he wouldn't have admitted that he was going to call her later if she hadn't phoned him. Her next problem was what to wear. She had an aqua cotton-knit sweater that she'd been more or less saving for a warm day and a special occasion. Since this offered both, she decided to wear that and her best-fitting jeans.

There were more than three hours to kill before it was time to meet Johnny, and she thought it would be a good time to begin her paper on *A Separate Peace*. Although she'd been riveted by the book, writing about it wasn't easy, and she'd been putting off the assignment all week. At least she could get started. Then there was always laundry to do, a necessary bore, or taking pictures for the alumnae magazine. She was responsible for candid shots of students and wanted to have a large collection of prints to show to the editor, who would make the final selection.

Faith was mulling over the order in which she should accomplish all these activities when she heard Dana and Shelley stirring. Dana had flung off the covers and was beginning her early-morning exercise routine and Shelley was blinking at her watch. "It's after nine o'clock and I have to eat breakfast and be at swim practice by ten. Help!"

"I have until eleven to get to Oakley. Bret's in the semi-finals of the tennis tournament and needs me for moral suport," Dana said.

"What are you doing, Faith?" Shelley asked, stumbling out of bed.

"Who knows?" Faith answered.

"Well, I personally think you're crazy if you don't call Johnny."

"Really, Shel?" Faith was leaning on her elbow, watching Shelley and Dana.

"What have you got to lose?" Dana gasped between sit-ups.

"You're the only one who hasn't had a real romance. Here's the perfect opportunity," Shelley pointed out.

Faith couldn't repress a giggle, and Dana looked at her suspiciously. "Is there something you're not telling us?"

"Whatever makes you say that?" Faith started laughing.

"You called him already, didn't you?" Dana guessed.

"I did," Faith admitted, sheepishly.

"And you let me go on like I was writing an advice-to-the-lovelorn column!" Shelley said. Then she picked up her pillow and aimed it at Faith, who ducked just before it grazed her head.

"You're a terrible liar." Dana laughed and shook her head.

Shelley was halfway out the door on her way to the bathroom, her towel slung over her shoulder, when she stopped and smiled at Faith. "I really hope it works out with you and Johnny."

"Ditto," Dana asserted.

"That makes three of us," Faith said, and then added softly, grateful for their support, "and thanks."

CHAPTER FIVE

When he saw Faith, Johnny leapt up from where he'd been sitting on the low brick steps that led to the entrance of Baker and grasped both her hands in his. They smiled warmly at each other. Faith had been ready for a half-hour but had restrained herself and arrived outside the dorm on the dot of noon.

"Been here long?" she asked, slowly withdrawing her hands from his.

Johnny appraised her five-foot-ten frame approvingly and then muttered, "Just as I remembered."

"What did you say?"

"Nothing . . . I mean I did get here about fifteen minutes early. For some reason I had trouble concentrating this morning."

"That's funny, so did I. I must have re-

written the opening paragraph for this paper
I'm writing — or rather *not* writing — a
dozen times. I loved the book, *A Separate
Peace,* but writing the report is agony. Anyhow, it's too nice out to worry about that
now."

"I'm with you. It's not a day for worrying.
How about you taking me on a walking
tour?"

"You've never been here before?"

"A couple of times for a play or concert,
but I've never really cased the grounds in
the daytime."

"Let's have our picnic first, and then I'll
take you around."

"Good idea. These sandwiches and sodas
are weighing me down." Johnny showed her
the brown paper bag he was carrying.

"And my contribution might atrophy in
the sun." Faith was cluching a bag filled with
pretzels and a plastic container of mustard.
"Come with me to the picnic grounds, otherwise known as the skating pond."

They strolled leisurely along the path behind the dorms, and Faith pointed out the
sports complex and the tennis courts. Faith
nodded or smiled to the few kids she passed,
and then they bumped into Alison Cav-
anaugh, who made a point of stopping and
being introduced to Johnny. Faith was especially pleased to have Alison, the dorm housemother, meet Johnny. Only recently Faith

hād complained to her that she wās worried
that she'd never meet a boy she'd like as anything but a friend, and Alison had assured
her not to worry and when it happened it
would hit her like a ton of bricks. Faith had
told her that was storybook romance stuff,
but now she wasn't so sure.

When Alison hurried off, moving like ā
racehorse, her mop of reddish brown hair
highlighted by the sun, Johnny remarked,
"That must be the youngest and best-looking
housemother in captivity."

"And the nicest. You know, she's only
twenty-five." Faith added, "She single-
handedly made it possible for me and Shelley
ānd Dana to get along. In the beginning, we
had what amounted to an armed truce."

By the time they'd arrived at the "picnic"
grounds and settled down on a grassy knoll
beside the pond, Faith was describing in detail her hopes and fears about coming to
Canby Hall. She even told him how Canby
Hall had been founded in 1897 when thirteen-
year-old Julia Canby had died of fever. Her
father Horace Canby had opened a girls'
school on the property that Julia would have
inherited.

Johnny was such a good listener that they
had finished their sandwiches ānd were
working on the pretzels and mustard when
Faith realized she'd been talking nonstop
about herself.

"What about you?" Faith asked, slightly embarrassed at the way she had dominated the conversation.

"I think this combination is sensational." Johnny answered, munching on a mustard-dipped pretzel.

"I didn't mean the food."

"Neither did I."

She realized then that he was referring to the two of them, and her heart flip-flopped.

"What's your term paper about?" she asked, not wanting to get too personal.

"Hope you're ready for this," he warned her. " 'The Family's Role in Controlling Juvenile Delinquency.' That's an aspect of criminology that interests me a lot."

Faith, who had been so animated, suddenly looked grim.

"Something wrong with the subject?" Johnny inquired. "You look as though I said I was writing something to promote crime, not prevent it."

Faith remained silent and stony-faced.

"Come to think of it," Johnny reflected, "you got that same look on your face when I told you I wanted to be a detective. Do you have something against cops?" He was half-kidding, but his smile quickly faded when he saw how aloof she was.

"Faith, will you please tell me what I said wrong?"

"My father was a policeman." Her voice

was trembling, and Johnny knew he had touched on a painful subject.

"Do you want to talk about it?" Johnny was sure something terrible must have happened.

"My father was an outstanding officer and was awarded several citations for bravery. My mother was very proud of the recognition he'd received and had the citations framed and hung in the living room. People who came to the house always commented on them, but my father told them he was simply doing his job. Then one day when I was ten years old, the phone rang. I'd just come home from school and hung around while my mother talked. After that, everything was a blur, but I remember my mother finally trying to explain to me that my father had been killed on active duty in an attempted bank robbery. He received another award posthumously, but ever since I've hated those citations."

"I know how you feel, Faith, but your father died a hero."

"That's what my mother, my older sister, Sarah, and even my kid brother say, but I wish he'd never been a policeman," Faith said finally.

"He was willing to take risks in order to improve society."

"I don't think it was worth it."

"I guess I'm willing to take the same risks," Johnny said.

"But I don't want to get involved with someone who thinks that way." Faith spoke impulsively and immediately regretted revealing her feelings.

"Look, Faith, there's a long way to go. First I've got to get through high school, and then hopefully get into John Jay College of Criminal Justice. Then I have to rack up points in the police force that will qualify me to be a detective."

"How do you do that?" Faith asked, curious in spite of herself.

"The guidance counselor at my school told me becoming a detective depends on the number of arrests I can make as a cop — not just arrests for misdemeanors, which are small crimes like shoplifting and purse-snatching, but arrests for felonies — crimes of violence such as murder or armed robbery."

"You mean if you put your life on the line and survive, you might be promoted to detective," Faith scoffed.

"That's saying it like it is," Johnny conceded.

"Terrific," Faith said angrily.

"Hey, this is getting heavy. I thought we decided it was too nice a day to worry."

"We did decide that, didn't we?" Faith knew she had a tendency to be sullen whenever she thought about the circumstances of her father's death, and she didn't want to inflict her bad mood on Johnny. Faith crumpled up the brown paper bag, tossed it at the wire trash receptacle about ten feet away, and forced herself to stop reflecting on the past.

"Missed!" Johnny exclaimed, as the bag fell more than a foot wide of the mark. Then he scooped up the empty Tab cans and plastic container of mustard and pitched them into the litter basket.

"Three out of three. You're really a good shot," Faith chuckled.

"That's why I don't have to worry about being a cop."

"Please, Johnny," Faith pleaded, "let's not talk about that anymore." She slowly got up, walked toward the crumpled brown bag, and dumped it into the basket.

She kept on walking until she came to the edge of the pond and then stood silently gazing at the clear, calm water. In an instant, Johnny came to her side, gently placed his hands on her shoulders, and turned her around to face him.

"We won't talk about it until you want to," Johnny promised.

"Thank you," she murmured.

"And now, how about that walking tour?"

"You're on," she said. And as he pressed her close to him and lightly brushed his lips against hers, her worries evaporated.

Johnny was reluctant to let her go, and

Faith would have stayed in his arms indef-
initely, but common sense impelled her to
back away.

"What's wrong?" he asked ruefully.

"House rules," she explained. "If Miss
Allardyce, the headmistress, catches us, I'll
be grounded and you'll be banished."

"No kissing allowed on the premises.
That's a bummer. What about hand-
holding?"

"That's allowed!" Faith cried gleefully, and
they both broke out laughing at her un-
abashed enthusiasm.

"Show me the way!" Johnny ordered, and
firmly grasped her hand in his.

Faith proudly showed Johnny around the
campus, beginning with the chapel, where
they sat for a while and listened to someone
practicing the organ. Next, they passed the
headmistress's house, an imposing white
colonial with perfectly trimmed privet bushes
leading up the path to the door.

They backtracked so that they could visit
the library, which was deserted except for a
couple of kids who were taking books off the
open stacks or checking them out at the
front desk.

"I'll show you my favorite place to study on
rainy days," Faith said as she led Johnny to
the far end of the library. There were tables
of varying sizes against the windows, and
only one girl was there, poring over a book.

She looked up when she heard footsteps approaching.

"Hi, Mary Beth," Faith greeted her. "We keep meeting in the strangest places."

"Hi," Mary Beth replied, but quickly averted her eyes, indicating that she wasn't about to make small talk.

Faith sensed how uncomfortable she was, almost as though she'd been caught breaking a rule. Faith tugged at Johnny's arm and tilted her head towards the exit. She knew from past experience that it was futile to try and engage Mary Beth in conversation.

When they left the library, Johnny remarked, "That girl must be a real scholar. Either that, or she's hiding out."

"She's a mystery to everyone." Faith spoke with such finality that Johnny didn't pursue the subject.

"Where next?" he asked.

"There's the Main Building, where most of our classes are held, and next to that is the science building."

They walked hand in hand, neither of them feeling the need to talk. When they came to the end of the footpath, Faith started to turn back, but Johnny blocked her way.

"This has been one of the best days I've ever had," Johnny whispered.

"Me, too." Faith hadn't forgotten her private promise to stay away from anyone whose career might be dangerous, but it wasn't easy to deny her feelings. They held each other for minutes, oblivious of the world, until there was a rustling in the trees and loud voices.

Instinctively, Faith tugged at Johnny's arm, and the two of them plunged off the path and into the woods. When they were a safe distance away, they burst out laughing.

"Close call. I might have been exiled on the spot." Johnny was still gasping for breath.

"And my reputation might have been ruined," Faith giggled. Then she added on a more serious note, glancing at her watch, "It's ten minutes until five. I have to help set up a surprise party we're having tonight."

"I'll walk you to your dorm."

This time Johnny led the way, and when they arrived at Baker, Shelley was on the fourth floor, half-hanging out the window. "Faith," she shouted, "I've been waiting for you. Hurry up."

"What's wrong, Shel?" Faith could see, even from that distance, that Shelley was distraught.

"I can't announce it to the world. But come here, please!" Shelley's face was flushed.

"I'm coming, I'm coming," Faith yelled. Then she turned to Johnny. "I've got to run, as you can see."

"Do you want me to wait for you?"

"No, thanks. Sounds like she wants to keep it quiet. But I've really got to go now."

"Today was wonderful, and I think I'm . . ."

But Faith was already rushing into the house and could only guess the rest of the sentence. As she ran up the stairs, she hoped that the ending would be "falling in love." Then again, it might be something as innocent as "going to come back another time." But all speculations went out of her head when she saw Shelley frantically plowing through the contents of the drawers that she'd pulled out of her dresser.

"What in the world are you doing?" Faith asked.

"They're gone!" Shelley fumed. "They're gone! I left them in the top drawer, and I've looked through every inch of my clothing. They're just not here!"

"What are you talking about?"

"My bangles, the ones I just bought. Somebody swiped them!"

CHAPTER SIX

Faith knelt down and began folding the clothing that Shelley had recklessly strewn on the floor.

"Are you sure you put them in the top drawer?" Faith asked.

"Positive. I was half-asleep when I left this morning, but I remember seeing them when I grabbed my earplugs for swim practice. But just to make sure, I've pulled everything out."

"I noticed," Faith said, neatly piling up some sweaters.

"Do you think I should tell Alison?" Shelley asked gloomily.

"Not yet. Maybe someone borrowed them. None of us were here all afternoon, and it's possible —"

"Never. If someone borrowed them, they

would have left a note. I think there's a thief in our midst."

Shelley sounded so dramatic that Faith had trouble not laughing, but she wanted to say something comforting. "Well, whoever it is won't be able to enjoy wearing them, because then we'd see who the culprit is."

"That's for sure. But I'm still going to check out everyone's wrist!"

Just then Dana entered the room and caught the tail end of the conversation. "Did I hear something about a wrist inspection?" She waved her two arms in the air.

"Someone took my bangles," Shelley grumbled. "They were in my top drawer when I left this morning, and when I went to put them on about an hour ago, they were gone."

"Oh, Shel, that's awful. Is anything else missing?"

"I never thought of that."

"Me neither." Faith handed her a pile of socks and then jumped up and checked out the things in her dresser. Dana did the same, but neither of them discovered anything missing.

"Of course, I'm not what you'd call a neat-nik. Half the contents of my drawers would have to disappear before I'd notice it," Dana remarked.

"Same with me," Faith said. "I could be missing something for weeks and not even

know it. Shel's the only one who's totally
organized."

"Lot of good it does me," Shelley griped.

"Look, Shel, why don't you come with me
to help with the decorations for Heather's
party? It's going to be in Room 207, an after-
midnight secret pig-out. Her roommate Tracy
is planning the whole thing and wants to
make it a surprise."

"How'd you get roped into helping?" Shelley ordinarily would have encouraged Faith's
participation, but she was still mad at the
world.

"Tracy's the art editor on the *Clarion,* and
she asked me the other day when she was
messing around with my pictures for a layout
for the softball team story. Their other roommate, Ginny, is going to keep Heather out all
evening. They have a movie date with some
guys in town and won't get back until close to
twelve."

"Lucky them," Shelley sighed.

"Come on, Shel. You're good at decorating,
and it will take your mind off your troubles."

"Shelley, you should go," Dana advised.
"The best way to stop worrying is to get involved."

"This is a conspiracy, but I'm not going,"
Shelley said. "I want a chance to look around
and see who's acting suspicious."

"We'll call you Shelley the Sleuth," Dana
teased.

"Shelley the Sleuth," she echoed as she finished tidying up. "That does have a nice ring to it. If I knew what I was doing, I probably shouldn't have touched a thing until I'd taken fingerprints."

"I'll help you, Faith," Dana said.

"Let's get started then. I promised Tracy I'd be there at five, and I'm already late. She's bringing in plenty of junk food and we can fuel up on that and skip the Saturday night slops in the cafeteria, if you want, Dana."

"That suits me. Last time I dined at Canby Hall on a Saturday night, they had their pale yellow dinner. Everything, from the boiled potatoes, to the cauliflower, to the fish dish, had a pale yellow cast."

"What the dietician needs is your sense of color," Shelley said.

"Right," Dana agreed. "Food should *not* be monochromatic."

Dana and Faith had run down the stairs to 207 where Tracy, a trim girl with finely chiseled features and an air of authority, was directing Casey Flint, who was balancing herself on a chair, on how to thumbtack a roll of crepe paper.

"Thank goodness you're here. And you brought Dana. That's terrific," Tracy said.

"What's the big rush?" Faith asked. She was accustomed to Tracy's bossiness on the paper, but she wasn't the least bit intimidated by her. Also, she admired her ability to get things done.

"The party's not till late, but half my helpers are busy or have dates, and that's why I want everything done *before* six-thirty."

"Where should we begin?" Dana asked.

"There's a pile of balloons on my bed, and they're just waiting for you to start blowing, Dana. And Faith, you can tack the end of these streamers to the wall."

"Glad you guys showed," Casey said as she stretched toward the ceiling. "Cheryl Stein was supposed to be here to help with this detail, but she's already a half-hour late."

Casey was always glad to see Faith, who had helped her from running away from school a number of months before.

"It's not like her to fink out." Tracy frowned thoughtfully. "She was going to pick some flowers for our room and bring them over."

"You think one of us should go for the flowers?" Dana asked.

"If she's not here in fifteen minutes, I'll go myself," Tracy volunteered.

Tracy had been cutting the roll of crepe paper and handing the streamers to Casey.

"You look like an angel, Casey," Faith observed jokingly. "I should have brought my camera." Casey was anything but an angel.

"You'll be a fallen angel if you don't trade places with me soon," Tracy quipped.

"This is good for my figure," Casey said.

With that, she reached for a streamer, lost her footing, and came crashing down to the floor. In the process, she pulled down a dozen of the ribbons that had already been hung, and she lay on the floor, her arms and legs entangled in a colorful array.

There was a collective gasp from the three other girls. They hurried over to where Casey was sprawled on the floor and hurled questions at her. "Are you okay?" "Did you break anything?" "Can you move?" "Should we get a doctor?"

"My arm hurts, but I don't think I broke anything," Casey muttered, slowly pulling herself up to a sitting position and then taking inventory of the various moving parts of her body. She wiggled her feet and legs with increasing speed.

"Your lower appendages are in good working order," Faith observed, happily.

"Yep," Casey said, testing her arms. "But I am a fallen angel because my wing has been clipped." She held her right elbow with her left hand.

"Maybe it's broken," Dana suggested.

"You should go to the infirmary and have Zennie look at it," Tracy instructed. Ms. Zenger was the starched school nurse.

"Later. Right now, I'd appreciate it if you'd upwrap me." Casey smiled at how ridiculous she must look sitting in the middle of the floor entwined in ribbons.

"All we need is to surround you with tissue paper and put a bow in your hair, and you'd be the perfect human gift," Dana said.

Casey laughed at the image, but then looked around at the mess. "I really wrecked the place."

"Don't worry about that." Tracy helped her stand up and led her to an easy chair. "The three of us can get it together, and you can watch while *I* risk breaking *my* neck."

It was six-thirty before they slowed down, and Tracy called for a junk food break. They gathered around the easy chair and dove into the potato chips, Fritos, popcorn, cheddar cheese, and crackers, and complimented one another on what a spectacular job they'd done.

"Heather will be so surprised," Tracy remarked. "She's always the one who's planning things for everyone else."

"I better not tell her about my arm. She'll think she's responsible," Casey said.

"You really should go to the infirmary," Dana told her. "I'll walk you over."

"I'll go with you," Faith said.

"And I'll pick the flowers. We might as well give up on Cheryl," Tracy concluded.

"Never give up on Cheryl!" The voice came from the hall, and then Cheryl came into the room, slightly red in the face. Cheryl, who usually looked like an ad for Ivory soap, was disheveled. She was clutching two large bunches of flowers and while still holding them, collapsed on the bed nearest the door.

The girls stared at her, and in a chorus asked, "What happened?"

"Wait, don't say a word till I get some water for the flowers." Faith grabbed a plastic basket, sped down the hall, and came back a few minutes later with the "vase" filled with water. Dana immediately relieved Cheryl of the flowers and began arranging them.

"Tell us what happened," Tracy said.

"There was a small crisis in our room and that's why I'm so late."

"Go on," Casey urged.

"Well, I'm not sure I'm supposed to talk about it, but no one said not to, and . . ."

"Get to the point." Tracy, like everyone else, was getting impatient.

"I've been at Canby Hall four years, I graduate in June, and this is the first time I ever heard of anything like this happening."

"The suspense is killing us," Faith said.

"Well, I had planned to get here on time," Cheryl said. "But when I went to look for my best blue linen blouse — which incidentally I've been saving for some decent weather — it was gone."

"Gone," Dana repeated, and exchanged a knowing look with Faith.

"Maybe Lisa borrowed it," Casey suggested.

"No way. We have an unwritten agreement

that we don't borrow anything without asking. We've shared a double for two years, and neither of us has ever gotten into a hassle over clothing."

"Could it have gotten hidden under something or dropped off the hanger?" Casey asked.

"I've searched every inch of my closet, and the only thing I discovered was an old pair of sneakers that I've been missing since the first week of school. We even tore apart our dressers. The only possible conclusion we could come to is that it was stolen."

"Stolen! That's hard to believe," Casey said.

"I've never heard of that before." Tracy shook her head incredulously.

"Neither had we, but what else could it be?" Cheryl was resigned.

"That might be what it is." Dana made this remark so casually that she got everyone's attention. "Right, Faith?"

"Right," Faith answered without hesitation.

"You two sound so positive. Is there something you know that we don't?" Tracy asked.

Dana glanced at Faith questioningly, and Faith shrugged her shoulders.

"Shelley's brand-new bangle bracelets, that she bought yesterday, were missing from her top drawer today." Dana stated this as though she were on a witness stand.

"You're kidding!" Tracy exclaimed.

"I can't believe this," Casey said.

"I think we should report this to Alison right now." Cheryl straightened up, ready to do battle.

"But first we should get Casey's arm fixed," Faith said.

"Your arm? What happened, Casey?" Cheryl looked startled.

"I fell off the chair hanging the streamers. Nothing serious."

"I'm really sorry. You'd think losing my blouse was the end of the world, and here you are, suffering in silence."

"Don't be silly. I'm sure I'll live."

"First things first," Cheryl said. "We'll go to the infirmary, and then we'll meet with Alison."

The girls left the half-decorated room together, silently. They all felt uneasy but didn't discuss it. It was the first time for all of them that they had ever thought someone might be taking things at Canby Hall. It rocked their image of the school and of each other.

CHAPTER SEVEN

Alison was always available to the girls when she was "at home" and made a special effort to be around weekends. She did more informal counseling then, usually about problems with boys, than any other time. Therefore, she wasn't a bit surprised when there was a knock on her door shortly after she had returned from the dining hall.

She fully expected to see a lone girl on the verge of tears because the boy she was meeting hadn't shown up or even bothered to call, or a distraught freshman upset because some kids were going to the movies and hadn't invited her along. Alison was so comforting and sensible that problems that originally seemed overwhelming, became manageable.

Alison wasn't prepared to see five girls — two seniors and three sophomores — at her door, but she welcomed them. She had trans-

formed her attic apartment in Baker into a
warm, friendly suite of rooms decorated with
colorful posters, floor pillows, and comfort-
able chairs. As the girls plopped on the pillows or sank into the chairs, Alison noticed
Casey's arm was in a sling and naturally
thought that this was the cause of the visit.

"Tell me all about it," Alison said as she
passed around a large crystal bowl brimming
over with peanuts. She placed the nuts on a
coffee table, sat down, looked sympathetically at Casey, and waited for her to begin.

"Oh, this," Casey said, then briefly recounted how she'd fallen off the chair and
just returned from the infirmary where Zennie had assured her that nothing was broken
— the purpose of the sling was more of a
reminder to be careful than anything else.

Tracy spoke ominously. "That's not why
we're here."

"It's not?" Alison sat down slowly. "Why
are you?"

"It's up to Cheryl and Dana to tell you,"
Tracy said.

"For heaven's sake, *somebody* please begin," Alison pleaded.

"My blouse was stolen," Cheryl announced.

"And Shelley's bangles," Dana said.

"*Are you sure?*" Alison was known for her
remarkable ability to solve emotional problems, but this was something else. She tried
not to overreact, but she knew Baker's good

reputation, largely due to her unfailing interest, was suddenly threatened.

"We're sure," Cheryl replied.

"It can't be anything else," Dana confirmed.

Then the two girls elaborated on how, when, and where the loss had been discovered. Alison listened intently and remained silent after they'd finished, trying to grasp all the details.

"What do we do next?" Faith asked.

"There are two possibilities," Alison said. "We can call a meeting of the entire dorm and make a public announcement, or we can try to keep the matter quiet and see what develops. You could be wrong."

"Would a public announcement make the possible thief surface?" Casey asked.

"Probably not. In fact, it might have the exact opposite effect," Tracy remarked.

"But it might temporarily put a stop to her activities," Dana said.

"It also might scare a lot of the younger, more timid girls," Faith said.

"That's true. We don't want everyone running around looking at one another suspiciously," Dana said.

"For the time being, I think we should keep a lid on what's happened," Alison advised. "The six of us know, and Lisa and Shelley. That makes eight. There is an outside chance that this was just a spring-fever prank and everything will be returned."

"Or perhaps there'll be a wave of thefts. Then what?" Faith could be excruciatingly practical.

"Then, of course, we'll change our tactics." Alison was capable of seeing all sides of an argument. "I'll have to tell Miss Allardyce about this, however."

"But why?" Dana asked.

Patrice Allardyce was the demanding but aloof headmistress. She kept her distance from the girls, but was considered to be fair in her judgements.

"I have to report any serious problems to Miss Allardyce. Besides, she's probably dealt with this kind of thing before," Alison answered. "And to be perfectly honest, I haven't."

For the next hour, Alison chatted with the girls about everything but the problem. They all put the subject on the back burner until they drifted off — Cheryl to take a shower, Casey claiming exhaustion and the need to lie down, and Tracy wanting to finish cleaning up the room. Dana and Faith, once they were back in 407, immediately resumed their speculations about the real-life whodunit.

"We should be on the lookout at the party tonight. Whoever is guilty will know that the thefts have been discovered by now and might act strangely," Dana predicted.

"That's possible," Faith said.

"Or she might have such a guilty conscience that she'll confess," Shelley added.

"Maybe," Faith said, thoughtfully.

"Or as Alison says, this could be a kind of spring-fever madness," Dana said, still hoping it was all a joke.

"Actually, I think Alison's a lot more concerned about this than she's letting on," Faith said.

"You're probably right. All the more reason I'd like to get my hands on the person." Shelley shook her fists in the air and frowned ferociously.

Faith, sitting at her desk, cowered at Shelley's antics. "I hope so, too," she grinned, "not the least reason being that I don't want my roommate flipping out."

Shelley pulled out her knitting, an activity that she claimed was a great tranquilizer. "It makes you feel funny, doesn't it? I mean, someone here *stealing*?"

"I know," Dana said, "It never seems as if the *real* world can invade Canby Hall."

"Yeah," Shelley said, "except when someone gets kidnapped!"

Tracy had spread the word earlier that 207 was having a birthday party. All Baker "inmates" were invited, and were urged to be there at least five minutes before the stroke of twelve so that the birthday girl, Heather, really would be surprised. The curfew on

Saturday night was twelve o'clock, so all the girls, except for the ones who had gone home for the weekend, were expected to show. Though parties like this were supposedly secret, Alison was always aware of them and pretended ignorance.

For the next few hours Faith forced herself to work on her English paper, and Shelley wrote letters home. Faith completed the first draft of her paper, and although it was rough and rambling, she was pleased that she had something to work with. Shelley had written her two brothers, and a long letter to Paul. Dana experimented with three new styles with her long dark hair. Shelley, now twisting multicolored glass beads around her neck, watched Dana.

"You really think those go with that orange T-shirt you're wearing?" Dana couldn't help commenting on the garish combination.

"Come on, Dana. I've been so understated lately that I feel this great need to express myself. Besides, whoever liked those bangles will love these beads, and if I catch someone eyeing them hungrily, that might be a clue to —"

"Before this goes on much longer, I think we should get going," Dana suggested. "It's seven minutes till midnight."

"Ready," said Faith.

"Me, too," Shelley chimed in.

Dana held the door open for them and

then carefully closed it. They each seemed to understand that the closed door might discourage any further intrusion.

"Follow your ears," Shelley commanded, and led the way down the stairs where the music was blasting.

Room 207 was vibrating with the sound of New Wave and high spirits and loud exclamations about the fantastic decor. A huge cake with eighteen candles was sitting on Heather's desk.

By five to twelve the room was filled wall-to-wall with people. Tracy turned off the music, climbed on a chair, held up her arms, and pleaded for silence.

"Please, everyone, let's quiet down. Heather will be here in seconds. Somebody close the door so she'll really be surprised."

The manic noise was reduced to a faint hum; someone flipped off the light, and the crowd waited and listened. Then Heather's and Ginny Weissberg's footsteps were heard pounding up the stairs.

"Where is everyone?" Heather was saying, just outside the room.

"Who knows?" Ginny replied. Ginny — wispy, blond, and vague — was the exact opposite of Heather, and her answer was typical.

"This place is like a cemetery for a Saturday night," Heather continued. "I hope nothing's wrong."

With that, she opened the door, and simultaneously the lights were switched on and there were shouts of "Happy Birthday!" "Surprise!" "Hardly a cemetery!" "More like *Saturday Night Live!*"

The usually mature Heather momentarily lost her poise and was unable to speak.

Tracy charged over to where they were standing. "You really are surprised, aren't you?" she asked, beaming at Heather.

"I'm thunderstruck," Heather murmured finally. "Now I know why Ginny was stalling so much downstairs. She made me help her look for her sweater all over the place, including the reception room and the phone booth."

"I think whoever's planning to get here is here," Tracy decided, looking around.

"Maggie's gone back for her violin. In the rush she forgot it, but as soon as she gets here we can light the candles and sing 'Happy Birthday,'" Casey said.

Maggie was a tiny dynamo with frizzy red hair, and her violin-playing was renowned throughout the school.

"What's taking her so long, I wonder?" Cheryl mused. "She only lives two doors down the hall."

"She'll be here any minute. Might as well get started." Tracy pulled over the desk. Just as she was about to light the candles someone jostled her elbow so that her hand made a dent in the cake and messed up the frosting.

"Look what you made me do," she barked, pulling her hand away.

"I'm so sorry," someone whimpered.

Tracy looked up and saw that it was Millie who had stumbled and bumped into her. "Oh, it's you," Tracy muttered.

"I didn't mean it," Millie apologized. "I think somebody pushed me."

She looked so forlorn that Tracy's initial annoyance dissipated. "It's okay. It figures you'd mess up the cake," Tracy told her, and tried to repair the damage by smoothing the frosting over the dent with the cake knife.

Maggie burst into the room, her freckled skin an unusual pink hue, and cut through the crowd. She didn't say anything. Then she yelled, "It's gone! It's gone!" Her voice was so shrill that she could be heard above the sound of the music and dozens of heads turned to look at her.

"What's gone?" several girls asked at once.

"My violin."

"Where was it?" Tracy asked, trying to keep calm.

"I kept it in its case in the bottom of the closet. I played it yesterday afternoon, and I know I put it away. Somebody's taken it!"

With that she collapsed on a chair, covered her face with her hands, and burst into sobs.

Dana rushed over to Maggie, kneeled

down beside her, handed her a tissue, and whispered something that had a calming effect. Then she stood up and implored everyone to not let this spoil the party.

"I can't believe this could happen at Baker House," Heather groaned. "The best dorm at Canby Hall."

"One missing violin — it's not the end of the world," Maggie said. She obviously regretted making a scene and tried to make amends. Like many people with a short fuse, she had a remarkable capacity for a quick recovery.

"That's true," someone else remarked. "It's a violin — not the crown jewels that have been stolen."

"It's also my sweater," Ginny said. "I wasn't just stalling downstairs. I know I have a tendency to lose things, but I hadn't worn my green sweater in a while, and it was missing —"

"That makes *four* stolen items. There's got to be a thief!" Shelley blurted out without thinking.

The word *thief* circulated through the crowd like an electric current. That was all anyone could talk about, and by the time the cake was sliced and served, details of the thefts had become public knowledge.

Shelley was mortified when she realized what she had let slip out. She ran over to Dana and said, "I blew it. I blew it."

"It was just a question of time before the news broke. Maybe it's even better this way."

"I hope so," Shelley said. "Everyone will be more alert, anyways."

"That's right," Dana agreed, "and therefore it will be much more difficult for whoever it is to operate."

CHAPTER EIGHT

For the next few days there was constant whispering among the girls about who was the most likely suspect. The topic, which generated almost as much interest as the subject of boys, was not confined to Baker. The entire student body was caught up in conjecturing about who had taken other people's property, and why.

While everyone tried to joke about it, no one really thought it was funny. A girl at Canby Hall stealing things was hard to believe.

On Wednesday at assembly, which took place before breakfast, Miss Allardyce gave her weekly inspirational talk about what is expected of the ideal Canby Hall girl. The perfectly groomed headmistress, her hair in a French twist, was wearing an immaculate white shirtwaist dress with a black patent leather belt and black patent pumps. She droned on about the value of hard work, respect for achievement, the need for courtesy and kindness in the world.

Assembly was compulsory, the students attended with a minimum of enthusiasm, and they were only half-awake. There were five minutes left when Miss Allardyce began to speak about honesty. Then she subtly wove into her talk what everyone else had been discussing since Heather's party.

"As you know, secrets are hard to keep, and in a school like Canby Hall, where we are presumably very concerned for one another, when something unfortunate happens, the news is immediately telegraphed throughout the student body. You all know what I'm talking about."

The girls who had been half-listening were suddenly attentive. Stealing was a serious offense, and everyone was curious to know how the headmistress would react. Some believed she might ground the entire school until the girl confessed. Others thought she might ignore the whole issue, hoping it would go away.

All were convinced that once the thief was discovered, Miss Allardyce would make sure that she was punished or even expelled. Therefore the entire assembly was surprised at her final remarks: "The items that have been taken are precious to their owners, but the self-inflicted damage to the person committing the crime is immeasurable. Therefore, we are not going to call the police into this. We do have to consider the reputation of the school. However, the entire staff, including the maintenance people, have been alerted to keep their eyes open. If anything suspicious is seen, they are to report it to me immediately."

Then she gracefully stepped off the podium, leaving the girls more baffled than ever. As they crowded out of the assembly hall, everyone was trying to interpret the headmistress's message.

"What did all that mean?" Shelley asked. She was wending her way to the dining room with Dana and Faith. "I thought she'd be a lot tougher — maybe scare the kid into confessing."

"I thought she might try using bribery," Dana added. "You know, promise leniency if the guilty person comes forth."

"I guess she's hoping to achieve the same results without threats or promises," Faith surmised. "Self-inflicted damage is strong stuff."

"Depends who it is," Dana said.

"Personally, I have my own ideas about who's responsible," Shelley offered in an off-hand manner.

"Who?" Dana and Faith asked.

"There's only one person who wasn't at Heather's party. And even though she's anti-social, I think it's very odd that she didn't drop in for a minute."

"Who do you mean?" Faith was puzzled.

"I know who she means," Dana said.

"Who?" Faith repeated. "I can't think of anyone who wasn't there."

"That's just the point. She keeps to herself so much you wouldn't miss her," Shelley said.

Faith frowned thoughtfully. Finally she whispered, "You mean Mary Beth."

"You got it!" Shelley exclaimed. "And I'm not the only one who thinks so. That's all we talked about at swim practice yesterday. Actually, someone else brought up her name, but I had to agree that M.B. is probably the one."

They had arrived at the dining hall and took their places at the end of the cafeteria line.

"It's not fair to make accusations." Dana kept her voice low, not wanting to be over-heard.

"I'm not," Shelley retorted. "I'm simply telling you what conclusions the entire swimming team has come to. Anyone who has had any dealings with her thinks she's perfectly capable of such a thing."

"You need some hard evidence," Dana cautioned. "Just because someone's unfriendly doesn't mean —" She stopped in midsentence.

Two girls in line ahead of them turned around and unabashedly listened to their conversation. "Who do you think it is?" one of them asked.

"I think it's . . ." Shelley started to say. But before she could finish Dana squeezed her arm and at the same time said, "We don't know. Like everyone else, we're trying to figure it out."

The girls looked skeptical, but before they could ask any further questions, there was the sound of dishes crashing to the floor, and a heavy thud followed by a burst of laughter. The girls popped out of line to see what was happening.

"It's only Millie," someone said. "She's dropped her tray for a change."

"Poor Millie," Dana sighed as she saw her sprawled on the floor, in the middle of the orange juice, cornflakes, and milk.

Some girls helped her up and wiped her off with paper napkins. They giggled all the time, while Millie remained impassive. The one thing Dana was grateful for was that the incident had interrupted the discussion about the thefts. In order to keep off the subject, she asked about the food.

"Do the scrambled eggs look more rubbery than usual, or is it my imagination?"

"Safest bet is always cold cereal. Even the Canby Hall chefs can't ruin that," Faith said.

"I'll settle for vanilla yogurt and an orange." Dana pushed her tray along so that the curious girls were forced to move on.

Shelley was quiet and glum as she followed Dana and Faith with her tray to an empty round oak table in the far corner of the dining hall. Dana realized that she was responsible for Shelley's change in mood and wanted to explain.

"I'm sorry, Shel, for shutting you up like that. Even if you turn out to be right —"

"But you know what she's like. Walks around this place like she's too good for everyone. One girl on the swim team has a brother who asked her out, but she wasn't interested. And he was gorgeous, too."

That made Dana and Faith giggle, and Shelley's face brightened. "You see what I mean, don't you?"

"Yes, I know she is odd, but not because she doesn't want to go out with someone's brother," Faith said, remembering how strange it was to see her coming out of the phone booth, fully dressed, early Saturday morning, "but that doesn't mean —"

"Who's odd?" Casey placed her tray on the table and settled down in the chair next to Dana. She had taken her arm out of the sling to eat.

No one answered, and Casey repeated the question, staring expectantly at each girl. They remained silent, and Casey said, "You guys are like the sphinx, but I can guess who you're talking about."

"Who?" Shelley was unable to keep quiet any longer.

"Her initials are M. B. G."

"Told you so!" Shelley shouted.

"Everybody thinks it's her," Casey continued. "She's such a snob, and she's the only one in Baker who didn't come to Heather's party."

"Maybe she had reasons," Dana said.

"I can't imagine what they were. Someone passed by her room and she was sitting at her desk, reading. It's one thing to be a bookworm, but it's something else to hide behind your desk when everyone else is celebrating. She acts like a girl with a terrible secret."

"Like what?" Dana asked.

"Like she did something awful and doesn't want to face anyone." Casey seemed so sure of her ground that it was difficult to dispute her.

"Do you plan to do anything about it?" Shelley inquired.

"Someone said that we should search her room when she's not around," Casey said, "but that's a lousy thing to do."

"You can't do that!" Dana exploded.

"That's an invasion of privacy." Faith was equally disapproving.

"But if the stolen goods were found in her room, that would be proof that she's the thief," Casey persisted.

"Someone might plant them there, as incriminating evidence," Dana suggested.

"Why would anyone do that?" Shelley asked.

"Because someone wants to get her in trouble, and at the same time remove suspicion from herself," Dana explained.

"I never thought of that," Shelley admitted.

"Well, I'm not about to take drastic measures, although I did think about writing her an anonymous note," Casey said.

"What good would that do?" Dana couldn't see any practical value to poison pen letters.

"Let her know she's a prime suspect and press her into confessing."

"But if she's not guilty, that's really a mean thing to do. It'll just make her more nervous and withdrawn," Faith said.

"I'm not doing it, Faith. I just said it was an idea. But I'm sure going to watch her like a hawk." Casey stuffed some eggs in her mouth.

"Me, too," said Shelley. "Frankly, Faith, I don't understand why you're defending her. Remember how she acted when you wanted her to do the 'Historic Homes' story?"

"I can't forget that, and especially now because Judy Barnes told me yesterday that she's committed up to her eyeballs in extra-curricular stuff and she wants to get out of doing the story. Says she's got to spend some time cramming for her exams."

"What'll you do now?" Dana asked.

"Probably wind up doing it myself, but what I know about Boston would fit on the head of a pin."

"If Mary Beth had taken on the assignment, you wouldn't be having these problems. Why are you so tolerant and forgiving, suddenly?" Shelley said.

"To be perfectly honest, I had given up on Mary Beth." Faith spoke thoughtfully, and then she added, "But I know what it means to be an outsider. The more people treat you different, the worse you feel."

Shelley remembered how she, too, felt the first few weeks of school. Pine Bluff might just as well have been another planet, she felt so out of it being at school in the East.

"You forget how homesick I was in the beginning. If anybody looked at me cross-eyed, I felt like crying."

"But we got over it, Shelley. If we hadn't, you can see how easy it'd be to be dumped on," Faith said.

"I suppose so. That still doesn't prove she's innocent."

"My uncle's a lawyer," Dana said, "and he says that for his client to be convicted of a crime, the prosecutor has to prove beyond a reasonable doubt that the accused was guilty."

"I still think she's guilty." Casey remained adamant.

"And I'm still hungry!" Dana smiled and jumped up, hoping to dispel the gloom that hung over the table like a black cloud.

"I am, too." Shelley hurried with Dana toward the food line.

"If it's not Mary Beth, who do you think it is?" Casey was unable to let up.

"I don't have the foggiest idea," Faith said. "I'm just trying my hardest to stay neutral."

But Faith's determination to keep an open mind was sorely tested the next day. Ellie Bolton, a tenth-grader who shared a triple on the fourth floor, was a tall, self-possessed, willowy blond who had two passions in life — poetry and her boyfriend, Peter. Peter was in his senior year at a school in New Hampshire. At Christmas, Peter had given Ellie a gold heart-shaped locket hung on a delicate link chain. She had promptly filled the locket with Peter's picture, and she wore it day and night. The only time she took it off was when she was in gym, took a shower, or went running. Since getting out of bed in the morning in time for breakfast was a major operation, she was forced to squeeze in her running at off-hours, usually mid-afternoon when she had a free hour between classes. Thursday afternoon was one of those days that she had a break after her class that ended at two-thirty. She rushed back to Baker, changed clothes, and jogged along the less populated paths on the campus. Ellie had this activity down to a science, leaving exactly twelve minutes to shower, dress, and make it to class on time.

She had dumped her running clothes onto the bed and slid into her jeans and T-shirt at lightning speed. Then she reached for her locket that she had left on top of everything. For a second, thinking it must have dropped to the floor, she bent down to look for it. Then, with increasing panic, she pulled off the spread, shook the pillows, and tore off the sheets. Waving the bedclothes vigorously, she muttered to herself, "It's been stolen. I know it. It's been stolen."

She had less than three minutes to get to history class and didn't want to be late. Leaving everything in a mess, she grabbed her canvas bag, bolted down the stairs, and sped across the lawn, arriving breathless and red in the face just as the bell rang.

"You made it!" Dana said, as Ellie fell into her assigned seat in the back of the room. Dana and Ellie had become friendly ever since the second semester, when they found themselves seated beside each other and agreed that writing notes was often more interesting than paying attention to Mrs. Scott. Mrs. Scott, who had a mind like an encyclopedia, often went off on tangents about some obscure fact of history and in the process totally lost her audience.

"I barely made it," Ellie muttered.

"I can see you've been running, but you look wrecked. Maybe you're overdoing it."

"It's not that. It's something else. When I got back to my room —" Ellie broke off as Mrs. Scott gave her a long, cold look.

"What happened when you got back to your room?" Dana scribbled on a piece of loose-leaf paper and passed it over to Ellie.

"My locket was missing. Gone!" Ellie slipped the note back to Dana, who gasped so loudly that Mrs. Scott looked at her. Dana quickly coughed and cleared her throat, successfully disguising her sound of alarm.

As soon as class was over, Ellie resumed the conversation. "No one knows how much that locket means to me. I wouldn't have cared if she'd taken anything else. My watch is a lot more valuable, so why didn't that appeal to her?"

"I can't answer that, but I think the kids who really care should get together and see if we can't come up with something."

"Whatever you say, Dana. Right now I feel totally helpless."

"Be in my room at five o'clock. And I'll get all the others who are involved to be there, too."

CHAPTER NINE

Dana rounded up each girl who had been victimized, plus their roommates. Casey, when she heard about the meeting, volunteered to come because she thought she might be able to shed some light on the most recent theft.

"We need all the information we can get," said Dana when she encountered Casey. Dana was on her way to chorus and didn't have time to stop and talk. "Be in 407 at five." She hurried off and didn't return to Baker until everyone had already assembled in her room and was trying to come up with some common features about the thefts. About twelve girls were sprawled on the floor, the chairs and the beds.

Faith indicated an open place on the floor, and Dana sat down beside her without interrupting the conversation. "Whoever it is had an amazing instinct for zeroing in on what I cared about most," Maggie grumbled. "No other violin will ever be that special."

"So was my blouse. The only one I ever bother to have dry-cleaned," Cheryl said.

"And I hadn't ever worn my bangles. Do you suppose she knew that?" Shelley asked.

"Don't know. But my sweater was hand-knit by my great-grandmother," Ginny added. "She certainly has a good eye."

"Wonder if she knows how much my locket means to me," Ellie mused. "I know she can't be interested in Peter's picture."

"The one pattern that's emerging," Heather surmised, "is that she's taking objects that will be missed, but not necessarily because of their value."

"Are you suggesting that she's doing it to be mean?" Tracy asked.

"Possibly. Or maybe it's just coincidence."

"Maybe we should leave something out that would attract the thief and then hide in the closet," Dana offered with a straight face.

"You can be the one to hide in the closet," Cheryl said. "Personally, I have claustrophobia."

"But which closet?" Shelley inquired earnestly, causing everyone to dissolve in laughter.

"Let's be serious," said Cheryl, who had

been laughing the hardest. "I think we have to look for clues."

"You mean if I see someone wearing my sweater, I can be sure who took it," Ginny offered.

"Yeah, or I'll hear someone playing my violin."

"Of course that won't happen. But maybe we'll see someone hanging around someone's room, waiting to get in. Or skipping classes so they can be here when nobody else is. Or who knows what else," Dana said. "Casey, you mentioned something about the missing locket. What do you know?"

"I hate to be the one to point a finger, especially because it might not mean anything, but I did see someone coming out of Ellie's room."

"When?" Ellie asked.

"When you were taking a shower."

"I keep telling Ellie she takes too many showers," Tracy piped up.

"I didn't think there was anyone around when I was taking a shower," Ellie said, ignoring Tracy's remark.

"The dorm is usually empty in the middle of the day," Casey went on.

"What were you doing here?" Dana asked.

"I was excused from gym because of my arm, and you know the Canby Hall rule that is left over from the Middle Ages. If you have a physical excuse, you have to come back to your room. Like you might faint if you go to the library or sit outside."

"And you saw someone hovering around my room?" Ellie asked anxiously.

"Not exactly hovering. She was actually coming out of your room just as I was going into mine. I didn't think anything about it until I heard about your locket."

"Who was it?" Dana asked hesitantly.

Everyone held their breath, knowing the answer would be the equivalent of a noose tightening around the neck of a condemned person.

"It was Mary Beth," Casey said softly, fully aware of what she was implying. Then she quickly added, "But seeing her come out of your room doesn't mean she took the locket."

"Are you kidding?" Cheryl exclaimed.

"Well, it doesn't," Faith protested, "unless you saw her with the locket."

There was a rising crescendo of exclamations, theories, possibilities, and accusations. The noise got louder and the shouts angrier until Dana stood up and waited until all heads turned towards her. She had an air of calm authority which succeeded in quieting down the girls.

"Look," she began, "we're not from the Old West, forming a posse to string up a suspect without a trial. We're supposed to be democratic, and fair. Some of us are too hasty to make judgments, based on flimsy evidence. Let's be super careful before we start accusing."

There was a murmur of begrudging agreement, and although it was easy to agree with Dana's statement in theory, most of the girls wanted to confront Mary Beth directly.

"What do we do now?" someone asked.

"I think we should be sure not to leave our things around. We don't want to *invite* trouble," Heather answered.

"She's pretty good at opening drawers," Maggie growled.

Several girls laughed, but Dana remained serious. "Let's try and keep our heads. Remember, it's all of Baker against one. The odds are in our favor that she won't be able to take the pressure and will confess before the school year is over."

Dana sat down, and listened to the reaction to her brief comments. "I think she's right. We shouldn't jump to conclusions." "But it's so obvious that it's Mary Beth." "Why would she do something like that?" "Why would anyone?" "It's an act of hostility." "Maybe someone thinks it's funny." "I think we should offer a reward for the return of the stolen goods." "That's not a bad idea." "Probably wouldn't work." "Let's face it, the only thing we can do is wait and see." "And hope that she wants to play 'show and tell.' "

The speculations about who, when, where, and why were endless and lasted until the first dinner bell sounded. Then the meeting broke up, and Shelley, Faith, and Dana were left alone in their room.

"Do you think that session accomplished anything?" Dana asked.

"I think you-know-who looks guiltier than ever," Shelley remarked.

"I'm afraid you're right," Dana agreed. "What do you think, Faith?"

"It's hard not to blame her, even though we don't have proof."

"I have a feeling someone will come up with some very soon. A lot of people are waiting for her to make one false step," Shelley said.

"I'd hate to be in her position." Dana straightened her bedspread and puffed up the pillows that had been squashed.

"Me, too," said Faith, shaking her head.

"But if she's guilty, she's asked for it." Shelley wasn't very sympathetic.

"And if she isn't . . .?" Faith's words hung in the air, unanswered.

In spite of their efforts to talk about other things during supper, their conversation kept returning to the mystery. It was too compelling a subject to resist. But when they

returned to their room to study, they agreed
to put it on hold.

"If I don't memorize these irregular verbs
for French tomorrow, I may flunk the test,"
Shelley said as she sat down at her desk.
Then she smiled, "Except I know my flunking
days are over."

"And I have to finish my paper for English.
Otherwise, I, too, will have the distinction of
being the first member of my family to fail
a course," Faith said.

"You are very dramatic," Dana laughed.
"Neither of you will flunk anything. But I
have a term paper, which I haven't even
begun, comparing Hamilton's and Jefferson's
philosophies and I promised myself to start
writing up my notes tonight."

"Speaking of notes," Shelley said, "what do
you think of the idea to send one to M.B.
and —"

"I thought we weren't going to talk about
it," Faith cried.

"We promised," Dana added. She poised an
enormous book over her head as though she
was about to throw it right at Shelley.

Shelley ducked her head and giggled,
"*J'oublie, mes petites enfants.*"

They finally did settle down to work, but
less than fifteen minutes later Faith was
called to the phone. Since she spoke to her
mother on Sundays, unless it was an emer-

gency, it could only be Johnny. She was pleased that no one could see how her heart was pounding as she flew down the stairs to the phone.

"Hello," she murmured.

"You sound like you've been running."

"I was . . . sort of," Faith said.

"Am I interrupting anything?" Johnny asked.

"Not unless you call writing that same old paper for English anything."

"I'll get right to the point, because I know the rules about tying up the phone. I wonder if you'd go to the Boston Pops with me on Saturday?"

Faith hesitated. She wanted to go, but when she thought of Johnny as a potential cop she shuddered. She closed her eyes and thought, *I'm not marrying him, just going to a concert.*

"I'd love to. I've never been to the Boston Pops and I've heard about them all my life." Faith felt strangely frightened and happy at the same time.

"I'll pick you up at five-thirty and return you no later than midnight."

"Terrific," Faith said. "I'll see you then."

She climbed the stairs in a dreamlike state. She didn't notice Shelley and Dana staring at her as she moved slowly toward her bed and sank back on the pillows.

"I can guess who that was," Dana couldn't resist saying. "It's the first time I've seen you so spacey."

"Are you going to let us in on it?" Shelley asked.

"You already know who it was," Faith laughed. "And he's invited me to the Boston Pops this Saturday. It's going to take me awhile to get used to the idea."

"I don't really want you to suffer too much," Shelley teased, "but do you recall how you made fun of me when I had attacks of love-sickness with Paul . . . and Tom, too, I guess. I do believe you have an extreme case."

"You may be right," Faith admitted. "What do you suggest I do? I'm afraid I'm getting into a situation I may regret."

"Go with it," Dana said.

"Go with it," Faith muttered, and reluctantly returned to her desk, vowing to write three pages of her report before she thought about Johnny again.

Going out with Johnny was even more fun than Faith anticipated. She had finally finished her paper and was in a mood to celebrate. Deciding what to wear was a major problem, but after much deliberation and comments from her roommates, she settled on a pale blue blouse, a beige skirt, and sandals. When Johnny met her downstairs she was astounded to see that he was wearing the male counterpart — a light blue cotton shirt and chinos. They both grinned at the similarity, and Johnny remarked, "Two great minds!"

On the way into Boston, Johnny was fascinated to hear about the thefts at Canby Hall and hinted that in a couple of years he'd be better qualified to help find the villain. Faith didn't want to spoil the day with another discussion of the pros and cons of being a police officer, so she promptly dropped the subject and asked what they were going to do for the two hours before the concert began.

They decided to have a feast from the booths at Quincy Market and started out with a slice of pizza.

Faith recognized Millie at the next booth where pottery was being sold. Millie was stuffing broken pieces of a vase into her bag.

"I'll give you another one, kid," the bearded young man behind the counter was saying. "You didn't knock it over on purpose."

"It was my fault, and I can fix it," Millie told him.

Faith realized immediately that Millie must have broken the vase she bought and the man behind the counter wanted to replace it for her.

"Hi, Millie," Faith greeted her. "Need some help?"

Millie looked bewildered, surprised to see

anyone she knew off-campus. "No, everything's okay," she mumbled and raced off.

"Who's that?" Johnny asked. "She acts as though you scared her to death."

"That's Millie. I would have introduced you, but she didn't stay long enough. Poor girl, she can't ever seem to do anything right."

They continued walking along, and stopped to share a pita bread stuffed with a lamb concoction, then some cherrystone clams, and finally they sat on a bench in the rotunda where they polished off a bag of chocolate-chip cookies.

The Pops was everything Faith had hoped for. Symphony Hall was transformed into a garden, decorated in green tones, the orchestra seats replaced by chairs and tables. The music ranged from light classical to popular, including excerpts from Tchaikovsky's *Nutcracker Suite* and tunes from *South Pacific*.

After the concert, they drove slowly back to Greenleaf, Faith resting her head on Johnny's shoulder. He walked her through the Canby Hall gates exactly ten minutes before curfew. Outside the entrance to Baker, he wrapped his arms around her and kissed her firmly on the lips.

"Faith," he whispered, "this was one of the best times I've ever had."

"It was for me, too." She clung to him until someone approaching tactfully coughed. The moment of magic was over, and Faith was back to reality. Johnny Bates was going to be a cop. That was what was real and that was what Faith couldn't stand.

CHAPTER TEN

The whole student body was busier than ever and talk about the thefts simmered down after several days passed without any new incidents. The girls were more cautious about putting their most precious belongings in inconspicuous places and in closing their drawers and doors. Otherwise, life went on as usual. It was still generally believed that Mary Beth was guilty, but there was nothing anyone could do until she made a slip.

On Saturday, Dana was alone in her room, working on a report. After a couple of hours, she felt she needed a distraction and decided to wander down the hall in hopes of finding someone who was just as crazy as she was to behave like a workaholic on a gorgeous Saturday in May.

She idly made the window at the far end her goal and ambled down the hall, listening for signs of life. But every door was closed, and she couldn't hear the sound of a stereo, the clicking of a typewriter, the scratching of a pen, or even someone breathing. She had almost reached the window when she heard a muffled sob come from behind the last closed door. Dana knew it was Mary Beth's room even though she'd never been inside, and she froze.

There was not a soul around, and Dana could have easily tiptoed back to her room without anyone ever seeing her. She half-persuaded herself that anyone else would be grateful for an intrusion, but Mary Beth might be resentful or angry. If she couldn't respond to anyone under normal circumstances, there was no reason to believe she'd want to be seen under stress.

Dana softly stepped away from the door and headed for her room, but the sound of Mary Beth's crying hung on the air like a veil of pain. No matter how foolish, Dana couldn't turn her back on anyone who sounded so anguished. She took a deep breath and gently rapped on the door. The crying momentarily stopped, and a weak voice asked, "Who is it?"

"It's me, Dana, and I thought you might need something." Dana waited to be invited in, but after a full minute of silence — at least she hadn't been told to go away — she tentatively opened the door.

The room, like Mary Beth, was understated and decorated in good taste. A lavender quilt covered the carefully made bed, softly colored prints of the sea hung on the walls, and the shelves above the desk where Mary Beth was sitting were neatly lined with books. Dana noticed that a great many of them were collections of poetry.

Tears were streaming down Mary Beth's face, onto a letter that she held in her hands. Dana dug in the back pocket of her jeans for a pack of Kleenex and handed it to her. Mary Beth removed a couple of tissues, blotted her eyes, and blew her nose.

"Bad news?" Dana asked, tilting her head toward the letter.

Mary Beth didn't answer, but her eyes brimmed with tears again.

"I'm sorry," Dana murmured. "Is there anything I can do?" Dana had never seen anyone so distraught.

Mary Beth shook her head disconsolately, and Dana resignedly thought Mary Beth was consistent, anyway. She'd never volunteered any information before, so why should she now. Dana thought she might as well give up trying to get her to talk, and started to back out of the room. But then she saw a look on Mary Beth's face — a look of hurt, yearning, and a plea for help — and Dana couldn't bring herself to leave.

There was an easy chair next to the desk,

and Dana sank into it. She didn't know how to begin, or even if she should say anything, but she was convinced that she had to try. She remembered that Faith's mother had once told her that all the training she'd received as a social worker wasn't nearly as important as her feelings for the people she was dealing with, and that often her intuition helped her reach clients when everything else failed.

Dana braced herself, a little scared of Mary Beth's reaction, and then boldly spilled out what was on her mind. "Look," she began, "there isn't that much time left until school is over so I guess that's one of the reasons I had the guts to crash in here when I heard you crying. You don't have to tell me what's bothering you, but you might feel better if you did. It's none of my business, but does it have something to do with that letter?"

"That's only part of it."

"Only part of it," Dana repeated. She was amazed that she'd gotten any response from Mary Beth, and felt a little freer about pressing her to reveal more. "What else?"

"I've been here since September, and I don't have a single friend." She spoke softly and her lip trembled. "I have no one to talk to."

"Whose fault is that?" Dana asked gently. "You've hardly spoken to anyone since the first day of school."

"I know it's my fault, but you don't know what it's like to feel different."

"Maybe," Dana exclaimed, "but I know what Faith feels. She's one of the few blacks in the school and when she first came here she thought everyone expected her to be carrying a spear and practicing strange tribal rites."

For the first time, Mary Beth's eyes shone with a glimmer of amusement.

"I'm afraid of people's reactions, too, and that's why I try to be invisible."

"But if you don't talk to anyone, you make new problems for yourself." Dana thought she was being subtle, but Mary Beth picked up on what she meant immediately.

"You mean everyone thinks I'm a snob."

Dana didn't say anything, not wanting to add to her hurt, but her silence was an implied agreement.

"If you were ashamed of something, wouldn't you want to keep it a secret?" Mary Beth asked suddenly.

"I don't think I'd want to broadcast it exactly, but I think I'd feel better talking to someone I trusted."

Mary Beth frowned at the letter she was still clutching, and then looked steadily into Dana's eyes. "My father's in jail," she said evenly.

"In jail!" Dana gasped, unable to disguise

her shock. "But why — what — what did he do?"

"He embezzled funds from the firm where he was working."

"You mean he actually stole money?"

"He made a mistake and he knows it," Mary Beth said sadly. And then as if a dam had burst she poured out the story of how her father had worked fifteen years as an accountant in a small paint manufacturing company. He was a loyal, respected employee, but he was ambitious and wanted things for himself and his family that his salary couldn't provide.

"He'd already borrowed from the bank to pay off the mortgage on our house. Then he got the idea that we should have a swiming pool in the backyard."

"What did your mother say?"

"She was worried about the cost, but he convinced her that he could pay it on time, over a three-year period. He did the same thing about buying a car, clothes for us, and vacations. And pretty soon, all his salary was eaten up. In order to keep off the bill collectors, he started embezzling funds from his firm. A little in the beginning, but then more and more. He juggled the books, in order to keep his boss from finding out. The funny thing is, he didn't want any of these things for himself, just for Mother and me. I can't remember him ever buying any expensive clothes for himself, trying to impress people in his office. It was all for us."

"How awful that must have been for him," Dana said.

"It was. He figured things would get back to normal and he'd pay back the money and no one would know the difference. But that didn't happen. The bills kept increasing and he kept taking more and more of the firm's money. Eventually, he couldn't pretend to himself that he could ever pay it back, and he confessed to Mr. Zanbar, part owner and president of the company, what he had done."

"And Mr. Zanbar had him sent to jail?"

"Actually Mr. Zanbar is a very nice man, sort of a grandfatherly type. But he had no choice about covering up for my father, because there were other partners in the company and they had to be told."

Dana shook her head, trying to grasp the nightmarish tale. "How long is your father going to be in jail?"

"Last June he was sentenced to eighteen months. He has about six more to go."

"And your mother?"

"She's at home. She works in a publishing house."

"She must miss you!" Dana exclaimed.

"That's one of the reasons I didn't want to come to Canby Hall, but she wanted me to get away. And Mr. Zanbar, who I'd only met a couple of times, came to our house and urged me to go, too. He knows someone on the board, so he arranged for me to come here. I guess I tested well, and I had a good record. I'm here on a full scholarship."

"That's fantastic. You must be a brain."

"Not about life, I'm not. I can't seem to handle it, Dana. I love my father, but I'm so embarrassed about him being in jail. I've been terrified that everyone in the school will find out. I just wish the whole thing would go away. I don't want to visit him anymore, it's so unreal."

"But you just said you loved him. How can you not visit him?" Dana asked.

"It's so bad to have such a limited time together, with guards around, and our conversation probably being taped. He wants to hear all about what's happening in school, but telling him I got an *A* on a test seems so stupid when he's locked up."

"So you don't visit him anymore?" Dana couldn't believe it.

"It's too tough. Last week I was all dressed and ready to take the train into Boston, and then I got cold feet. I felt so guilty about not seeing him that I wrote a letter trying to explain. This morning I got this letter back."

Mary Beth, her hands shaking, offered Dana the crumpled piece of white paper. Dana hesitatingly took the letter, almost afraid of what it would reveal. She knew that refusing to read it would not only be

cowardly, but also be interpreted by Mary
Beth as a rejection. Her eyes skimmed the
tearstained page:

Dearest Mary Beth,

*I received your letter two days ago, and
that's all I've thought about. I made a terrible
mistake taking funds that I foolishly thought
I could return, and I am being punished by
having to serve time in prison. But nothing
has been as painful to me as your letter saying you think it's better for both of us that
you don't visit me.*

*The worst part of losing my freedom is
that I'm separated from you and your mother
— the dearest people in the world to me. I
was counting on seeing you. Now, to be de-
prived of your visits is the worst punishment
of all. Mother writes me that you are con-
tinuing to excel in your schoolwork. As always, you have made us proud.*

*Please don't take away one of the few joys
in my life — seeing you. It will make the next
six months bearable. I know how difficult all
this is for you, but some day it will be a bad
dream and our family will be together again.*

I send this with my deepest love.

Daddy

Dana was so moved by the letter, and her
feelings for Mary Beth, that she could no
longer hold back her tears. Mary Beth was

exhausted after sharing her secret with Dana, but she was emotionally relieved. She slid the packet of tissues that was lying on the desk toward Dana. Now it was Dana's turn to wipe away her tears and pull herself together. Still sniffling, she stood up and walked toward the window that overlooked the playing fields behind Baker. Mary Beth watched her and said shyly, "Thank you for being so understanding. I wasn't sure how you'd react."

"I *am* human," Dana remarked, and turned around. She smiled at Mary Beth, a little embarrassed by her tears.

"You won't tell anyone about me, will you?" Mary Beth asked fearfully.

"What happened hasn't been your fault, and you shouldn't act as though it is."

"What should I do? I've hated being so alone, but I've been afraid of getting close to anyone. If they find out about my father . . ."

"I think things will be easier for you if you let me tell Shelley and Faith. I guarantee you they'll feel just the way I do. Give them a chance. You can count on them to keep your secret."

"You really think so?"

"I know so."

"I feel so much better now that I've told you, I think you may be right about everything. What else should I do?" Mary Beth asked.

"It just so happens that Faith still needs someone for the 'Historic Homes' story. How about doing it?"

"I think I'd like to," Mary Beth said hesitantly and then added with a new confidence, "I *do* know a lot about Boston."

"Good! You've solved her problem."

"Now what I should do about seeing my father?"

"I don't know, but if you'll let Faith ask her mother, I'll bet she'll have some good advice."

CHAPTER
ELEVEN

Faith and Shelley responded exactly the way Dana predicted when she told them about Mary Beth. Shelley couldn't quite comprehend that she knew someone whose father was in prison, and she made Dana repeat the story three times.

"No wonder she acted as though she wanted to dive into the washing machine when she saw me in the laundry room the first week of school."

"Now we can understand why she's acted so odd about a lot of things. It's up to us to let her know we accept her," Dana proposed.

"That's what I think," said Faith, and Shelley nodded her head in agreement. "And it won't be hard. Once she lets down, it's easy to like her, and if she didn't have such monster problems, I think she could be a lot of fun."

"What about the thefts? Does she know she's a prime suspect?" Shelley inquired.

"No, she doesn't, and I couldn't dump that on her now. She's probably just as curious as we are. Also, I'm absolutely positive she didn't do it," Dana said.

"Then more than ever, we've got to find out who did!" Faith said.

With Dana's encouragement, Mary Beth allowed herself to enjoy being part of the 407 group. Thanks to Faith, she came to a decision about her father. Faith's mother had had experience dealing with families of people who were imprisoned, and there was no question in Mrs. Thompson's mind that visits from families were crucial to keeping up the morale of inmates. Mary Beth was still uneasy about seeing her father behind bars, but knowing that she had three friends who she could confide in gave her courage. Her first tearful reunion with her father, after their exchange of letters, was so gratifying to both of them that she knew she could have made no other choice.

Mary Beth still hadn't overcome her shyness with the other girls, but she vowed that if she returned to Canby Hall next year, nothing would prevent her from responding to anyone who so much as smiled at her. The fact that she considered returning for her junior year was proof of how much better she felt about herself. Whenever she felt lonely she dropped into 407. Shelley, who had exhausted the patience of her roommates because she needed so much help with French, enlisted M.B.'s aid — now they all called her M.B. as a term of affection — and Mary Beth was delighted to be of help.

Mary Beth was feeling particularly high after a late night session when she had successfully drilled Shelley on the use of the subjunctive. Shelley was enormously grateful, as were her roommates, who praised Mary Beth for her saintlike patience. The dorm was quiet, and Mary Beth decided to take advantage of the showers being empty and after leaving 407 returned to her room for her towel and soap. She put on a robe and slippers, and then padded down the hall to the bathroom.

She smiled to herself, thinking what a good sport Shelley was to accept her roommates' teasing. As the water cascaded over her, she was almost tempted to sing, realizing that if it hadn't been for Dana she'd still be miserable. When she turned off the water and grabbed the towel that she'd left on the bench inside the stall, she was surprised to hear voices. Two girls were obviously standing over the sinks brushing their teeth because their words were muddled. They knew someone was in the shower but were indifferent to being overheard.

"I don't think there's any question," one girl said. "Just because she's hanging out at 407 doesn't mean she's innocent. I think that's probably a cover-up."

"The most damning evidence is that Casey saw her coming out of Ellie's room when no one was around. I don't see why Alison or Allardyce don't question her." The voice was cottony but the words stung.

Mary Beth stood paralyzed, the towel draped around her, her heart heavy as stone. *It's me they're talking about, it's me. They think I'm the thief.* She remained still until she heard the faucets turned off, footsteps retreat, and finally a door slammed. Then like a robot she finished toweling herself dry, slipped on her robe and slippers, and without any thought ran to room 407.

The girls were getting ready for bed when Mary Beth appeared. Dana had just popped a nightshirt over her head and was the first to see her framed in the doorway. "You look like you've seen a ghost," Dana observed.

Shelley, who was tidying up her desk, glanced in her direction. "Don't tell me they've turned off the hot water and you had to take a cold shower or that Millie flooded the bathroom again."

"What's wrong?" Faith asked.

"Do you think it's me, too?" Mary Beth forced out the words in a raspy monotone.

"Think what's you?" Dana frowned at her serious manner.

"That I'm the thief."

"No . . . never . . . What makes you say that?" Faith was disturbed to see that Mary Beth looked stricken.

Dana maneuvered Mary Beth toward her bed, and Mary Beth sat down on the edge. "I heard two girls talking about me. They think I'm guilty because Casey saw me coming out of Ellie's room when nobody was around, the day her locket was stolen. But I was there to pick up a book that was three weeks overdue in the library. I'd taken it out in my name and Ellie had borrowed it."

"And promised to return it," Faith guessed. "And she forgot."

"That's right. And I kept asking her and she kept forgetting, so I decided to do it myself. It was Hemingway's short stories and was on the reserved shelf, and I knew a lot of other kids were waiting to read it. I didn't bother to tell Ellie, but I guess I should have." Mary Beth covered her face with her hands and her body shook with sobs.

Dana patted her consolingly on the back, and Faith said, "Look, M.B., we know you're telling the truth. And Ellie certainly will stand up for you, if it comes to that."

"That's right," Dana agreed. "But I think we've been too laid-back about all this. You guys may think I'm really off the wall, but tomorrow I'm laying a trap and if all goes well, I'm going to catch the thief in the act."

"That would clear my name," Mary Beth sighed, using her towel to wipe away the tears. She was comforted knowing they were on her side.

"How you going to do it, Dana?" Shelley asked.

"Even though you may laugh," Dana began, "I'm going to lie in wait in the closet. Tomorrow there's a special assembly to discuss graduation. We're on our honor to attend, and I'll just be a little late."

"Or perhaps miss it altogether," Faith commented. Then she quickly added, seeing how serious Dana was, "But you'll be serving a higher purpose."

"Right." Dana was relieved that so far they weren't putting her down. "The criminal thinks the dorm is deserted and will go into action."

"What's going to lure the thief into our room?" Shelley insisted on learning the details.

"As you know, everyone's been careful about closing the door to their room. Well, I'm going to leave ours partially open."

"And what are you using for bait?" Faith asked.

"Shelley's feather earrings. I'm going to leave them on her dresser and they'll be *irresistible* to anyone who's looking for something odd to steal!"

"Especially if it's a girl with rather quaint taste," Faith quipped.

"Don't you think it's a good idea?" Shelley looked worried.

"Might work," Faith admitted.

"Then maybe you'll thief-sit with me?" Dana was heartened by Faith's response.

"I really have to be at tomorrow's assembly because I'll be taking pictures for graduation and I have to know all about the procession and the program and where the photographers will be standing and . . ."

"Okay," Dana muttered, crestfallen, "I get the message."

"Personally, I don't think you should do it alone," Shelley commented.

"You mean you'll do it with me?" Dana eyed her hopefully.

Shelley hesitated and then said, "I think it might be kind of fun to play cops and robbers."

"Terrific!" Dana exclaimed.

"And I'll cover for you at assembly," Faith offered. "If anyone notices you're missing, I'll say you were held up."

"That may be truer than you think," Shelley said, grinning.

"Don't get carried away, Shel. We're not dealing with an armed robber — just petty thievery," Dana said.

"You never know," Shelley said. "But now I think we'd better get some sleep. Have to keep our wits about us and not fall asleep while lying in ambush."

"Isn't it reassuring to know we've got the equivalent of James Bond and Sherlock Holmes on the case, M.B.?" Faith asked. She wanted to cheer up Mary Beth, who still seemed so forlorn. Her eyes were puffy and her skin was blotchy from crying, but she stood up and managed to smile wanly.

"What's really great," she murmured, before heading for the door, "is that I have you three."

The next morning there was the usual grumbling about having to attend assembly before breakfast. Shelley was louder than anyone in voicing her opinion and made sure that everyone in Baker was aware of her displeasure. Before she got dressed she went into the hall and buttonholed any girl who came within two feet of her, stating the sacrifice she was about to make for the glory of Canby Hall: listening to a speech on an empty stomach!

Her roommates were afraid she was over-doing it, and when she was getting dressed, Faith said, "You might as well put up a sign — ROOM 407 WILL BE VACATED FROM 8 TO 8:30! LIGHT FINGERS WELCOME!"

"I just want to make sure that everyone knows we won't be 'at home' during that period, and they're welcome to enter, browse, and steal."

When the warning bell rang, the Baker girls drifted out of their rooms and down the stairs, most of them still half-asleep. Shelley and Dana stayed quietly in their room until the dorm was empty. Dana had carefully placed the earrings on an otherwise perfectly bare dresser. They stood out like a beacon light, as Shelley said, "Just begging to be swiped."

Then she half-closed the door, while Dana squashed herself behind the clothes in her closet. Shelley squeezed in beside her, managing to step on Dana's foot in the process. Dana let out a muffled yelp that sounded more like a frog croaking, and Shelley practically choked trying not to explode in laughter.

The closet was pitch black except for a sliver of light that came through the crack in the door that Shelley had left open for breathing purposes. There was no room to move and the first five minutes of confinement seemed more like five hours. Shelley, whose ability to sit quietly and not talk was limited under the best of circumstances, began twitching.

"Be still," Dana breathed. "You'll ruin everything."

"I'm trying," Shelley whimpered, and made a superhuman effort to think about the last time she went sleigh-riding with Paul, her mother's homemade cornbread, and whether she should work in her father's drugstore over the summer.

She wasn't sure she could last another two seconds when there was the sound of the door to the room creaking open. Dana heard it, too, and clutched her arm so hard that she had difficulty not crying out in pain. *This is the moment I've been waiting for,* Shelley thought, *and the ordeal will soon be over.* She could hear Dana breathing faster and faster and knew she was just as excited.

They both listened hard, trying to follow with their ears footsteps crossing the room. But there was no sound, and they thought perhaps they were imagining things. Then they heard a definite thump coming from the direction of Shelley's dresser. The sneaky thief, once she determined the room was empty, probably relaxed and became a little careless about making noise.

Shelley, her heart racing like a steam engine, knew this was the moment of truth. She nudged Dana with her elbow, and indifferent to the clatter of the hangers and the fact that she almost fell flat on her face stumbling over the shoes on the floor of the closet, she plunged into the room. Dana followed her, and the two of them stood momentarily frozen, trying to get their bearings, blinking rapidly as they tried to adjust to the blinding sunlight that poured into the room.

"We know you're here, so why don't you give up?" Shelley tried to sound fierce, although she wasn't sure anybody besides Dana was listening.

"We heard you," Dana growled. "And you're not going to get away with this any longer."

Their eyes adapted to the brightness, and they looked around the room, mystified.

"I heard someone, I know it," Shelley said.

"I did, too. The door definitely creaked and then there was a noise, like someone zeroing in on the bait." Dana shrugged her shoulders, unable to explain the culprit's vanishing act.

Shelley edged slowly toward her dresser to see if there were any clues. She was half-afraid that someone would pop out of a drawer or through the window to attack her. But the window was open less than six inches, and not even Houdini could have slithered through that. She was within a hairbreadth

of her destination when she let out a scream.
"Someone *was* here! There's only one earring
left!"

"This is crazy!" Dana exclaimed.

"Why would anyone steal one earring?"
Shelley had gotten on her hands and knees
and was peering under the dresser thinking it
might have dropped.

"Maybe when the thief got up close, she
was too dazzled by their beauty to go through
with it," Dana said, as she walked toward the
door, intending to search the corridor for
signs of the escapee.

"Very funny," Shelley groaned, and leaned
on her bed to pull herself up. She stopped
midway and began giggling. Her giggle became louder, and soon she was laughing so
hard that she couldn't stand up.

Dana quickly backed into the room. "Have
you flipped out?" she asked, turning around.
And then she saw the cause for Shelley's
bizarre behavior, for there was the "thief,"
nestled in the bedclothes, playing with the
feather earring, and totally indifferent to the
commotion she had caused.

"It's Doby! It's Doby! Doby!" Dana cried out
the name as though she couldn't quite believe
what she was seeing. Then she too had an
uncontrollable giggling fit, fell on her knees
beside Shelley, and tried to grab Alison's
adorable cat. But Doby eluded her grasp,
leapt off the bed, and bolted out the door.

The two girls were still laughing hysterically when the bell rang, which meant assembly was over. They slowly got to their feet, knowing they'd miss breakfast if they didn't leave right away.

Shelley held up the mutilated earring. "The sacrifice I made," she said, looking at it wistfully.

"But now we know where to look for your bangles, the violin, the blouse, the sweater, and the locket." Dana tried to keep a straight face.

"That's right," said Shelley. "Doby's probably stashed everything away in her penthouse retreat."

"Undoubtedly," Dana agreed.

Then they had another irrepressible laughing jag before they finally managed to leave the scene of the crime.

Faith and Mary Beth waited outside the dining hall to learn if Shelley and Dana had been successful. Once they heard about the escapade, the hilarity was contagious and the four girls could barely get through breakfast without cracking up. Every two minutes they mentioned Doby, a feline they now endowed with superhuman qualities. Mary Beth was able to enjoy the story, for she had gotten over the initial shock of the conversation she had overheard in the shower. She kept assuring herself that no matter what people thought, she wasn't guilty, she had three friends who believed in her, and it was just a question of time before her name would be cleared.

CHAPTER TWELVE

On Saturday, June 1, Mary Beth awoke and had to fight off a not entirely unexpected feeling of depression. It was exactly one year since her father started serving time in prison. She tried not to dwell on the horrendous moment twelve months ago when Melvin Grover was sentenced by the judge. Now that the anniversary of that painful day had arrived, Mary Beth didn't want to talk about it. It was not a question of being secretive, but raking up old coals accomplished nothing, and she thought it was a burdensome subject to her friends as well as to herself.

She was happy when Faith suggested they go into Boston that morning and make the rounds of some historic buildings for the *Clarion* story. It would be the perfect distrac-

tion. As soon as they had breakfast, Faith
arranged with Mr. Bowker for the *Clarion* to
give them an allowance for their transporta-
tion into Boston and around the city, and
with the kitchen to provide a brown-bag
lunch.

They felt both carefree and independent as
they boarded the bus, cameras slung around
their necks. Mary Beth had borrowed a *Guide
to Boston* from the library and Faith picked
up a sightseeing map in Greenleaf near the
bus stop. On the way into the city they planned
their "attack" for the day, and decided to follow along the Freedom Trail, which the guide-
book described as a two-hour walk covering
"two-and-one-half centuries of America's
most important history." With each place
they visited, one of them would read aloud
the description. And although the *Clarion*
assignment was on houses, they couldn't resist investigating other historic landmarks.

They sat on the Boston Common, the old-
est park in the country, munching on their
sandwiches and people-watching. Every type,
from Hare Krishna dancers and mimes to
toddlers playing in the playground and elderly
people sunning themselves to lovers holding
hands, was part of the scene. After finishing
their sandwiches and Tabs, they treated
themselves to an ice-cream cone and made
their way to Beacon Hill, where they took

pictures of the landmark houses of Louisa May Alcott, Edwin Booth, and Julia Ward Howe.

They were mentally exhilarated but physically exhausted when they climbed into the bus that would take them back to Greenleaf, and they both dozed off. When the bus arrived, they felt refreshed and pleased with themselves. They talked all the way to Baker, congratulating themselves on having accomplished so much in one day.

Mary Beth had been totally absorbed in the project, and was relieved that she had survived the anniversary of the blackest day of her life without it being the downer she had anticipated. There were still six hours left, but she knew she could get through the evening, maybe go to the movies with anyone in 407 who was interested.

She and Faith trudged up the stairs to the fourth floor, and as she went down the hall to her room Faith called after her, "Come on in as soon as you're ready. We'll bore whoever's around with our historical savvy."

"Be right there," Mary Beth said, hurrying. She smiled to herself, still not quite able to believe that she was accepted, that she had friends who really wanted to be with her.

She dumped her things, ran into the bathroom to wash up, returned to her room to change her shirt and comb her hair, and then headed for 407. She knew Faith would be telling whoever would listen about their day, and Mary Beth couldn't wait to add to the story.

Mary Beth could hear the low voices of the girls as she came into the room, but the conversation stopped as soon as they saw her. Three sets of eyes stared at her uneasily, and Mary Beth knew she had been the subject of their discussion.

"What's wrong?" she asked, looking around at each girl, her eyes finally resting on Dana. She felt closest to Dana and expected her to answer.

Dana was lying on her bed, a Boston paper spread out beside her. She sat up and slung her legs on the floor when Mary Beth continued to look at her. "Might as well tell you," Dana said grimly, "since the entire school knows by now."

Mary Beth could feel her knees turn liquid and she fell into Dana's desk chair, which was just inside the doorway. "Knows what?" she asked weakly, even though she already knew the answer.

"It's all here, in black and white," Dana murmured. She folded the paper, strode across the room to hand it to Mary Beth, and pointed to a column headed "*A Year Ago Today.*" Mary Beth steeled herself and skimmed the items:

> *The Boston Red Sox set a record
> for stolen bases in one inning.*
>
> *The graduation speaker at Harvard, a member of the Federal government, was booed during his commencement address.*
>
> *Three hundred people trapped by an electrical fire in a twelve-story office building near Boston's Old City Hall were heroically rescued by firemen.*
>
> *Melvin Grover, accountant for the Zanbar Corporation for fifteen years, was sentenced to eighteen months in prison for embezzlement.*

Mary Beth was stunned into silence and read the item through three times before she finally looked up and mumbled, "Has everybody seen this?"

The other girls glanced at each other, but no one said anything.

"I already know the answer to that one," Mary Beth said, her voice breaking. "You did say the entire school knows by now."

"It was bound to come out, sooner or later." Dana gently took the paper away from Mary Beth and shoved it in the trash basket beside her desk.

"It doesn't really change anything," Dana tried to reassure her.

"You can't help it if your father's a crook," Shelley exploded, and then turned crimson with embarrassment when she realized what she'd said. She babbled apologies, until Mary Beth came to her rescue.

"I know you didn't mean that the way it sounded," Mary Beth said softly. Then she added in a whisper, "Even though that's what the whole world thinks."

"But once they learn the circumstances, people will understand why he did it and feel sorry for him," Dana commented.

"But who's going to explain that?" Mary Beth asked.

"I am . . . I mean I already have . . . I mean anyone who's asked me, like Maggie who came running in here with the article, I've told," Shelley said.

"You mean Maggie discovered the column and couldn't wait to tell you?" Mary Beth insisted on learning the details, no matter how painful.

"I guess I talk too much," Shelley muttered, as she avoided her roommates' glances.

"You suffer from hoof-and-mouth disease," Faith quipped.

"It's okay," Mary Beth said, "I really do want to know what happened today and what the kids are saying. How else can I defend myself?"

"You're right, M.B. There's no point in protecting you, and we might as well tell all,"

Dana spoke slowly and thoughtfully. "You begin, Shelley."

"I already have," Shelley laughed self-consciously, and then went on to describe in detail what had transpired after Maggie spotted the item in the newspaper.

"Of course she told Casey, and the two of them told us," Dana continued.

"A few minutes later some kids from the other floors made a point of letting us see the column. It wasn't so much that they were being mean. It was more like they thought of you as a celebrity," Shelley explained.

"I didn't know so many Canby Hall girls read the paper," Mary Beth groaned bitterly.

"Well, I told every one of them that your father had just wanted good things for his family and he *had* confessed to what he had done," Shelley said.

"Now you know absolutely everything, why don't we change the subject?" Dana suggested.

"I agree. I think we should all live it up," Shelley asserted, anxious to talk about anything that wasn't serious. "Let's do something special!"

"I know just the thing!" Dana said. "Oakley Prep is having a carnival tonight to raise money for its scholarship fund and Bret is on the committee. He wants me to meet him there and bring anybody I can get my hands on. A lot of other Canby kids are going."

"That sounds great. I promised I'd call Johnny when I got back from Boston. He wants to see me tonight, and I'm sure he'd go to Oakley," Faith said.

"What about you two?" Dana looked at Shelley and Mary Beth. "It should be a lot of fun, and you certainly want to help me endear myself to Bret."

"What are friends for?" Shelley asked. "How about it, M.B.?"

Mary Beth hesitated, torn between staying alone in the dorm or facing a world that now knew her secret.

Dana, as though she could read her mind, urged her to come. "You can't hole up in your room forever, M.B."

"That's right. The longer you wait, the harder it will be," Shelley observed. "I'll ask Tom to go and bring a friend for you."

"And we'll be around to give you moral support," Faith added.

Mary Beth, looking more like she was agreeing to go to her execution than to a carnival, said, "I'll go."

"Excellent!" Shelley exclaimed. "Now I have to figure out what to wear. I think my shirt with the clowns would be perfect. Okay, Dana?"

"Anything goes at a carnival," Dana conceded, smiling.

"I have to call Johnny." Faith grabbed some

change from her bag and rushed out of the room.

"And I'll call Tom," Shelley added.

"Let's plan to meet downstairs in twenty minutes," Dana said. "This should really be fun."

"Sure," Mary Beth said, trying hard to smile and not letting on that more than ever she'd just like to disappear.

The atmosphere on the vast Oakley Prep campus was charged with excitement. Japanese lanterns hung on poles were strategically placed on the lawn, which took on the aura of a lush velvet green carpet. Taped music seemed to magically filter through the surrounding trees. A variety of junk food stands, festooned with colorful ribbons, offered everything from cotton candy to frozen Milky Ways.

The girls from 407 and Mary Beth joined forces with a pack of others who made their way to Oakley. Dana immediately found Bret, who was at the table where tickets were being sold. He leapt up when he saw her, kissed her on the lips, thanked her for recruiting so many customers, and told her to have a good time until he could tear himself away. Faith then found Johnny engrossed in pitching balls at a row of wooden milk bottles. The purpose was to knock down as many bottles as possible and the reward was a free throw for every five bottles that were leveled.

Faith observed him without him noticing, but after a few minutes, she spoke up. "At this rate, you'll be here all night."

He turned around and dazzled her with his smile. "No, I won't," he said, tossing the ball behind him and grabbing her arm.

Shelley and Mary Beth, with Tom and his friend Richard, had been watching and they all moved away together. Shelley rattled on about how she couldn't wait to try some of the rides, and her enthusiasm made Mary Beth seem shyer than ever. Johnny, without knowing any of the reasons, sensed Mary Beth's discomfort and interrupted Shelley.

"Let's not just talk about it. Let's do it." He authoritatively led the way to the Ferris wheel where the sound of shrieks was deafening.

After waiting in line, Shelley and Tom climbed into the double seat ahead of Faith and Johnny with Mary Beth and Richard behind. Mary Beth, up until then, had been going through the motions of enjoying herself. But when the wheel started to revolve, and she felt herself suspended in air at the top of the arc, she shouted as loud as anyone else, a combination of fear and delight. Richard clutched her arm so hard that when the ride was over Mary Beth could see the imprint of his fingers. They giggled at how ridiculously fearful they'd been on an under-sized Ferris wheel.

They wandered around like kids in a candy store, trying to decide what to do next. Lots of Canby girls, caught up in the mood, smiled at them when they passed by, and Mary Beth's anxiety about being looked at as some kind of freak slowly disappeared. It wasn't until she stopped to buy a frozen Milky Way bar for herself, while Shelley, Tom, and Richard were checking out a stuffed animal booth, that she was sharply reminded of her problems.

Ellie, who had her hands filled with six candy bars, was backing away from the counter when she noticed Mary Beth.

"You're just the one I wanted to see!" she shouted.

"You wanted to see me?" Mary Beth asked apprehensively.

"Yeah, for two reasons. I read about your father, but I don't think that proves anything. And I'm sorry about not returning the book. Didn't mean to get you in trouble."

Mary Beth wasn't sure how the two things were connected, and was about to ask when someone yelled, "Ellie, how long does it take you to buy a candy bar? We're fading away."

"I'm coming!" Ellie called, and scurried off, leaving Mary Beth totally baffled. Ellie wasn't hostile or angry. If anything, she acted friendly and apologetic, and Mary Beth tried not to worry.

The couples continued walking and bumped into Dana and Bret, who lured them into taking a ride on the whip. The six of them piled into cab cars that whirled around with increasing speed. The ride lasted less than five minutes, but it was long enough for them to lose their equilibrium. When they climbed out, dizzy with the frenetic motion, they staggered around and then collapsed on the ground. They alternated between attacks of vertigo and laughing fits.

"Best thing is to walk it off," Johnny suggested.

"Whatever you say," Shelley complied.

"I'll set the pace," Faith offered.

"Just remember, we're in a weakened condition," Dana said, leaning on Bret.

Faith and Johnny led the way and the others followed, slowly recovering their balance. They edged themselves into a small crowd surrounding a trampoline and were just in time to see Cheryl finish her turn with three perfect somersaults.

There was wild applause and the good-looking, muscular Oakley boy who was obviously in charge said, "That's a tough act to follow. Who's willing to try?"

After a lot of muttering: "You do it." "No, you." "But you're good at it." "I just ate."

"That's no excuse." "I will if you will." "But I won't."

"Somebody's got to be brave enough," a voice shouted above the crowd.

Then a small figure, holding a cotton-candy cone above her head like a banner, wormed her way through the crowd, kicked off her shoes, and climbed onto the trampoline. "I'm brave enough," she announced, looking around for approval and taking some tentative warm-up springs.

"It's Millie!" Shelley gasped.

"I don't believe it," Dana said.

"Someone should hold that cotton candy for her before —" Faith began.

"Too late," Mary Beth groaned, as the startled spectators saw Millie leap into the air, misjudge her landing, and tumble to the ground.

Fortunately her crash landing was cushioned by grass, and after several kids helped her up, it was clear that no serious damage had been done. She was still clutching the cotton candy most of which had gotten stuck in her hair, which now glowed with small globs of pink.

It was hard not to laugh, but Millie shrugged off the crowd's reaction, seemingly indifferent to the scene she had created, slipped on her shoes, and walked away without a backward glance.

Mary Beth was having too good a time the rest of the evening to worry about anything. She and Richard hit it off so well that Faith and Dana had to remind them when it was time to leave.

Bret gallantly drove the girls back to Canby Hall, even though it meant he had to sacrifice being alone with Dana. They arrived at Baker within seconds of their midnight curfew, charged up the stairs to 407, and then talked about the carnival, boys, life, love — everything.

They apologized to Dana for messing up her love life by accepting Bret's offer to drive them back to school, agreed that he had administrative qualities that guaranteed his future international fame, and teased Mary Beth about her new conquest. The "instant replay" of all that happened was almost as much fun as the original.

Shelley threw herself on her bed and gazed at the ceiling. "It used to drive me nuts that I liked Tom so much. I mean I always worried which one I liked more, Tom or Paul, but now — now I just accept it. I love them *both*. So what?"

"Tom is awfully nice," Mary Beth said.

Shelley agreed. "And he understands that I want to be an actress, want to go to New York and study acting. Paul may *never* understand that."

By the time Mary Beth returned to her room and got ready for bed, the "A Year Ago Today" column had lost its terrible significance and had already become a dim memory.

CHAPTER THIRTEEN

The carnival spirit carried on through Sunday when the phone rang first thing in the morning. Tom and Richard asked Shelley and Mary Beth to a post-party cleanup, engineered by Bret. Bret had invited Dana and volunteered to pick up the three girls.

"Your first step towards international fame," Dana giggled.

"Never heard of a cleanup party," Mary Beth told Shelley after accepting the invitation.

"It's an offer we couldn't refuse," Shelley laughed. "We're going to be paid off in frozen candy bars."

Faith was feeling a little out of it, listening to her roommates talk about their plans for the day, when she was called to the phone. It was Johnny, asking her to the beach.

She knew she shouldn't, knew she was encouraging Johnny while she still had so many conflicting feelings, but she found herself saying, "I'd love it. But it's kind of cloudy."

"I'm an optimist, you know. Be ready in half an hour, with bathing suit, towel, and sunglasses! I'll be outside the front gates."

"See ya," Faith said, hung up, and ran up the stairs to get ready.

The minute she entered the room, Dana observed, "You're seeing Johnny, right?"

"You guessed it," Faith said, unable to stop grinning.

"And I bet he didn't invite you to clean up his backyard, which some boys seem to consider a privilege," Shelley groaned good-naturedly.

"We're going to the beach," Faith told her. "Give me a chance to break out my bikini, although it looks like it might rain."

"What about Richard?" Dana asked Mary Beth. "Bret tells me he's really a brain. He's also very handsome."

"He's shy, compared to Tom, who's the personality kid. But I think he flipped for M.B.," Shelley said.

"What makes you so sure?" Mary Beth asked.

"It's true, M.B. I know the signs. For starters, he couldn't take his eyes off you," Shelley said emphatically.

"Really?" Mary Beth was eager to hear more.

"And when Faith dragged us away before we turned into pumpkins, he looked like a sick puppy."

Mary Beth smiled self-consciously, then purposely got the attention off herself by asking Faith which beach they were going to. When Faith told her they'd probably go to Sandy Beach, Mary Beth's smile vanished and she got a faraway look in her eye.

"What's the matter?" Faith asked.

"Nothing, really. It's just that every summer since I can remember I used to go there with my father. Not this summer though . . ."

"We all have to cope with changes that we have no control over," Faith remarked.

"I guess I shouldn't complain," Mary Beth said, knowing that Faith was thinking she'd never see her father again.

"You never know what the future will bring," Dana said. "Now that my father's got a new wife, our relationship will never be the same, no matter how hard we try. And he's going to be in Hawaii for a year, too."

"Hey, isn't this getting heavy for so early in the morning?" Shelley said. "We're supposed to be having fun."

"You're right," Faith said.

Then Dana added, "Not only do you have a way with boys, Shel, but you've got Iowa horse sense."

Shelley's eye twinkled because she knew, although they teased her constantly, the girls really loved her, and Dana had paid her a genuine compliment. Her ego had been bolstered to the point where she decided to pick out her own outfit for the day. Without another word, she pulled a pair of chartreuse cotton pants and an orange plaid shirt out of the bottom drawer of her bureau.

The three girls watched speechless as she tugged on the pants and buttoned up her shirt. Then she turned to them for approval.

"Well?" she asked expectantly.

The silence was painful, but finally M.B. said tactfully, "I've never seen anything like it."

"Perfect for the job you'll be doing," Faith commented.

"It's what the well-dressed roustabout *should* wear," Dana said.

"Good," Shelley said, interrupting their remarks as unqualified approval. One was never certain if Shelley was as naive as she appeared. But one thing was for sure — she'd changed the mood from serious to frivolous, and she smiled when the girls agreed that when it came to coordinating colors, there was no one like her.

Faith was the first one to be picked up, and Johnny was waiting for her at the main gate when she arrived. She climbed in beside him in the Toyota, and they both started talking at once. After a few minutes they realized that neither one was listening, and they began to laugh.

"It's amazing," Johnny remarked, as he revved up the motor. "I've seen you less than twelve hours ago, and there's so much to talk about." He started to put his arm around her.

"I know," Faith said, sliding away from him into her neutral corner. She was fully aware that they were in front of the gates of Canby Hall. "Do you realize where we are?"

"All too well," Johnny replied. He determinedly placed his two hands on the steering wheel and took off.

They breezed along the highway, the forty-minute ride seeming much shorter as they talked about their summer plans, the pros and cons of boarding school, the advantages and drawbacks of being an only child.

"Next Friday, let's celebrate our first meeting at the Tutti Frutti," Johnny suggested. "Not exactly moonlight and roses, but I'll always remember it."

Faith hesitated, but then said, "I'll be there at four, right after my last class." She liked Johnny . . . too much.

"What are you thinking?" Johnny asked, sure that it would be something romantic.

"I was thinking," Faith said, unable to express her real feelings, "that I can't wait to try out some of their more exotic flavors, perhaps a combination of bubble gum, grape, and banana."

"You're lying," Johnny said. "You were thinking something much more romantic."

"You're right," Faith admitted. Then they both laughed and Johnny held her hand until they arrived at the beach.

Johnny parked the car in the self-service lot. Then they ran to their separate dressing rooms, changed into their bathing suits, dumped their beach bags on the sand, and hand-in-hand dashed toward the water where the waves were pounding the shoreline.

Johnny stopped at the edge and shook his head firmly. "I didn't think it would be this rough. I'm a terrible swimmer," he shouted above the roar of the ocean.

"Doesn't matter," Faith yelled back. "I'll show you how it's done."

She swam a little ways out and then gracefully dove beneath a towering wave. She ducked under the crest of several more, while Johnny watched her admiringly. She rode a wave into shore, and full of high spirits, impulsively threw her arms around Johnny and hugged him.

"Come on in," she insisted.

"Okay," he shouted, gritting his teeth.

The next thing she knew, a gigantic wave took them unaware and knocked them both down. Faith recovered quickly, but it took her almost a minute to see Johnny trying to get his bearings. He was floundering several yards away, his arms and legs flailing in the air. Faith ploughed swiftly toward him and grabbed him around the waist, and they swam toward the shore. For several minutes they stretched out on dry land, breathing heavily.

"We both forgot to duck, but I didn't see that monster coming," Johnny apologized.

"Me, either," Faith gasped.

"Maybe *you* should be the cop, you're the lifesaver."

Just as he said that, there was a blinding streak of lightning, a loud clap of thunder, and then the skies darkened dramatically. The two lifeguards who were situated along the beach on high ladder chairs that commanded a view of the ocean, blew their whistles nonstop until all the swimmers were out of the water. Then they hurriedly put up red flags, indicating the beach was closed.

It didn't take much convincing to get people to move because the rain had started, slowly at first and then with increasing speed. Soon it was coming down in torrents. There was an air of excitement, mixed with a sense of danger, as Faith and Johnny bolted for cover. They grabbed their beach bags along the way and found shelter in a picnic area that had redwood benches and tables covered with a tin roof. Along with dozens of other "sunbathers," they watched the storm play itself out.

When the rain was reduced to a light steady drizzle that showed no signs of letting up, Johnny conceded that it wasn't a perfect beach day. "I owe you one," he told Faith.

"It was fun anyway," Faith assured him, thinking that everything took on a special glow with Johnny, even a torrential rainstorm.

"Faith," Johnny said suddenly. "I have to tell you something."

"You sound so serious," she said, feeling frightened.

"I was accepted at John Jay."

Faith glowered at Johnny. "How long have you known about this?"

"I found out yesterday," Johnny replied.

"Why didn't you tell me? We've been alone all morning, so you can't say you didn't have a zillion opportunities."

"Because I didn't want to ruin our day. Bad enough that we're rained out at the beach —"

"Don't be funny."

"Okay, Faith," Johnny said, no longer apologetic or attempting to keep it light. "I know it's a subject that drives you bananas, and I just avoided it."

"The most important news in the world to you and you wait hours to tell me," Faith sputtered.

"I wanted today to be special, and to be perfectly honest, I've been so excited ever since I opened the letter I didn't want anyone — especially you — to discourage me. I understand how you feel about cops —"

"But you obviously don't understand how I feel about you!" Faith exploded and headed for the lockers.

"Faith, wait, I'll drive you home."

Her tears, mixed with the rain, spilled down her face all the way back to school. The usual bustling town of Greenleaf seemed as deserted and forlorn as her spirits. She wasn't sure how the day, which had started out so deliciously, had turned into such a bummer.

When they reached the gates of Canby Hall, Faith said, "You can leave me here." She opened the car door and got out.

"Faith, please, let's talk," Johnny begged.

"There's nothing to talk about. I don't want to be in love with a cop."

Johnny smiled. "You said you loved me!" He was happy in spite of himself.

"That's my problem," Faith said and ran up the path to Baker House.

CHAPTER
FOURTEEN

Faith had managed to avoid telling her roommates about her fight. Actually, it was so one-sided — she was the one who was mad. On Monday, she went through the motions of attending classes, doing her assignments, talking with her friends, but her heart was heavy.

Johnny was constantly in her thoughts, and she only wanted to be alone. She was grateful to be in study hall, where talking was forbidden, and she could give in to her mood of despair. Who was it that said, " 'Tis better to have loved and lost, than never to have loved at all." *Not true*, Faith thought. She wallowed in self-pity and made herself feel worse by dwelling on the fact that everyone else's love life was running smoothly. Even Mary Beth had admitted that she really liked Richard. He was the first boy she could talk to about poetry and not feel dumb. Faith was genuinely happy for Mary Beth, but that blossoming romance made her fading one more painful.

What Faith didn't know, as she chewed on her pencil and stared out the window, was that at that very moment Mary Beth was suffering. Although she had had a wonderful time the day before with Richard, and no one had made the remotest reference to her father being in jail, the discussion in biology class sharply reminded her of her situation.

She was only half-listening to Mr. Farber, who was going on about whether genetics or environment was more important in forming character, but then he mentioned the word *criminal*. The word itself triggered a rush of emotion, a combination of fear and embarrassment. "Based on several studies, it has been shown that crime runs in families. Would someone like to comment on that statistic?" he asked.

One girl's hand shot up and he nodded toward her. "Okay, Barbara, what do you think?" Barbara was glib, quick, and got to the point immediately.

"I think criminal tendencies run in families, just like blue eyes. They're inherited characteristics."

Mary Beth sank down lower in her chair,

convinced that the remark was directed at her. Dana, who was sitting in the row behind, could see her friend flinch and tried to rescue her. Without bothering to raise her hand and be called on, she spoke up. "That's crazy. There's no such thing as a 'break the law' gene. It all has to do with environment. If you're hungry and don't have any money, you'll steal to survive."

"Not if you have good genes, you won't. You'll get a job," Barbara countered.

"That's not true," Dana said.

"I agree with Barbara," someone else piped up. "It's in the blood."

The arguments flew back and forth with everyone contributing, except Mary Beth who kept her head bent and her eyes down. She could barely make sense of what anyone was saying. When someone mentioned embezzling, she gripped the sides of the desk so hard that her knuckles turned white and she thought she might pass out.

The ordeal ended when the bell rang, but Mary Beth stayed glued to her desk until everyone had cleared out. Only Dana hung back and urged her to move. "Come on, M.B. You'll be late for our next class."

Mary Beth stood up and moved slowly toward the door. "I guess I was kidding myself that the worst was over," she murmured as they left the room. "Everyone knows about my father and thinks I'm a criminal."

"That's not true. It was a general discussion, and you're taking it too personally."

"No one knows who stole the things from Baker, and everybody thinks it's me. I was actually looking forward to coming back to Canby Hall next year, now that I have you and Faith and Shelley for friends, but now I don't want to. . . ." Her eyes filled with tears.

"You've got to come back next year. Since you didn't do anything wrong, there's no reason why you should run away."

But Mary Beth was too distraught to see the logic of Dana's thinking and muttered, "It doesn't matter whether I'm guilty or not. What matters is that everyone thinks I am."

Then, before Dana could say anything else to convince Mary Beth that she was being too sensitive, the warning bell rang and they both had to rush off.

After supper later that evening, when Dana and her roommates were alone in their room, settling down to do their assignments, she recounted the biology discussion and Mary Beth's reaction.

"Even though Farber summed up the arguments by saying that there really is no scientific evidence of genetic criminal tendencies, M.B. thinks everyone is pointing their finger at her."

Faith, who had been so preoccupied with her own problems, was more concerned about somebody else for the first time in twenty-four hours. "We've got to do something for M.B.," she said.

"But what?" asked Dana. "Whoever is doing the stealing is very tricky. Doesn't leave clues and hasn't stolen anything lately. She probably figures that if nothing else is taken by the time school is over, she can go home without ever being discovered."

"I don't know what we can do," Faith despaired. "But whatever, we've only got three weeks to do it in."

"Eighteen days to be exact," Dana corrected her.

"And if we don't find out who it is, M.B. says she's not coming back," Shelley told them.

"This is awful," Faith said, summing up the desperate situation in three words.

"Maybe we should ask someone who's totally outside the school to help us," Shelley suggested.

"You mean bring Scotland Yard in on the case?" Dana inquired.

"This is no time to kid around," Shelley said. "But now that you mention it, why don't you ask Johnny what we should do, Faith? He wants to be a detective, you said."

Shelley was shaken when she saw how Faith was affected by her remark. There was a look of pain in her eyes, and her voice was barely audible. "That's probably a good idea, Shel, but I don't think I can ask him."

"Aren't you speaking to him?" Dana couldn't hide her surprise.

Faith, who did not enjoy being secretive, was relieved to tell in detail all that had happened on Sunday. But she was a little taken aback when both Dana and Shelley took Johnny's side, and she couldn't dismiss their remarks lightly.

"It's his career, not yours," Dana said. "You practically forced him not to tell you he was accepted at a college specializing in criminal justice."

"He didn't want to upset you on one of your last times together before summer vacation," Shelley said.

Faith thought about what Shelley and Dana said. "Well, I did come down hard on him, but I meant what I said. I don't want to be in love with a cop. I'm sure about that."

"Okay," Dana said. "You're entitled. But at least tell him in a civilized way. Don't just throw something like that at him and run. That's just mean."

"What should I do? Call him and make a date. What?"

Shelley said, "You said you made a date with him for next Friday. Keep it. Meet him and tell him in person what you feel."

Faith laughed ruefully. "What makes you

think he'll show up after the way I treated him?"

"You just have to take the chance," Dana said.

Then, although nothing had been solved about M.B., and Faith had serious doubts that Johnny would appear on Friday, she felt much less alone since she'd talked to Dana and Shelley. During the next few days, whenever her resolve to keep the anniversary date weakened, her roommates gave her courage.

On Friday, Faith tried her best to stay cool and not take any pains with what she wore. The usual jeans and T-shirt. No reason to dress for a meeting that might never take place and was really a good-bye.

Faith fidgeted through her afternoon classes and when the dismissal bell rang, she hurried to 407 to dump her books and took off for town. She forced herself to walk at a reasonable pace. No point in rushing for a meeting that might consist of herself and an ice-cream soda.

All the way to Greenleaf, in order to stop worrying about whether Johnny would be there or not, she kept her mind occupied by trying to recall the twenty-six of Tutti-Frutti's flavors named after each letter of the alphabet. Almond, Banana, Caramel, Dutch Apple, Eggnog, Fudge Ripple, Ginger, Hawaiian Punch, Island Fruit, Jelly Bean . . . She was halfway through the list when she reached the village. As casually as possible she walked to the ice-cream parlor, which was doing its usual bustling hot-weather business.

Faith walked inside and looked for Johnny among the customers lined up to make their selection. She was about to give up on his being there when she glanced into the back room and saw him sitting alone in a booth, staring at an untouched double scoop of strawberry ice cream in front of him. Also on the table was what looked like Faith's favorite, a combination of maple walnut and pistachio mint. She quietly slid into the seat opposite him and whispered, "Hi. Looks like you were expecting me."

He looked up slowly and his previously glum expression changed into a grin he could barely contain. "I was hoping, not necessarily expecting. No fun celebrating an anniversary alone."

Faith felt a tightening in her stomach, but she knew she had to be honest with Johnny. "Johnny, listen, I didn't come to celebrate our anniversary."

Johnny's face became serious. "Why did you come, then?"

Faith took a deep breath. "I came because I wanted to tell you in a calm, considerate way what I shouted at you last week. I mean . . . that I do love you but that I can't, *can't,* have a cop as a boyfriend. I'd be miserable, frightened, angry, all the time."

Johnny looked down at his melting ice cream and pushed it around with his spoon. "I guess I understand how you feel but I can't agree with you, and I sure don't like it. Faith, the world is full of all kinds of danger. Danger for yourself and people you care about. You can't avoid it."

Faith was thinking what new arguments she could present when there was a loud commotion in the front of the restaurant.

"Bad news," Johnny said in a low voice, sizing up the situation.

There were screams of hysteria. Terrified customers shouted, "They've got guns!" "Help!" "Don't kill us!" "Don't hurt my children."

Faith, panic-stricken, turned around and saw two muscular, tough-looking, spike-haired young men holding guns. One, his arms covered with tattoos, guarded the door, which he'd locked. The other, who resembled a giant ferret, stood in the center of the front room and motioned with his gun for the two terrified girls who had been scooping out orders to come out from behind the counter.

"Shut-up, everybody, and do what I say," Ferret-face ordered. He waved his gun threateningly in the air, and the volume of the screams increased.

"I said shut up!" he roared.

Johnny slowly stood up, held his arms in the air to show he wasn't carrying a weapon, and moved toward the front room.

"Let's do what he says." Johnny's low-pitched voice and calm manner restored a small sense of calm to the horrified customers.

"Who do you think you are?" the punk at the door asked, looking at Johnny.

"You let me do the talking, remember, Tattoo?" Ferret-face growled at his partner, who scowled but didn't say anything. Then he turned to the others. "We're just holding you hostage for a while. And while we're waiting for our terms to be met, we'll have one of our friendly neighborhood holdups."

There were more exclamations of panic. A young woman shrieked, and a toddler in a stroller began wailing. Then Johnny's steady voice could be heard above the noise of the fifteen terror-stricken people. "Take whatever you want, just so no one gets hurt."

"What are you, some kind of wise guy?" Ferret-face pointed his gun menacingly at Johnny.

"Trying to keep things cool," Johnny answered without flinching.

Faith, her mouth dry and her hands clammy, was paralyzed with fear but couldn't help being awed by Johnny. She wanted desperately to help him, but she couldn't do it. *These guys look like killers,* she thought. *The only way to get out of this is with help from outside.* She knew the owner, Mr. Leeds, whose crusty manner belied the fact that he loved kids, was a marshmallow inside, and didn't own a gun.

"Where's Leeds?" Ferret-face asked. He had checked out the store earlier to learn the owner's name.

"Here — I — I'm here," the balding, middle-aged Mr. Leeds, his brow covered with beads of perspiration, muttered. He had sunk into a chair in the corner, and looked like he wanted to blend into the wall.

"Get up, Baldy. I want you to call your wife."

"My — my wife. Wh — why?" he stuttered.

"Because I want fifty thousand dollars, that's why. And I want it in cash."

"Fif — fifty thousand. That's my life's savings."

"That's what I figured." Ferret-face smirked proudly. "Now, just go to the phone, which I see is on the back wall over there, and tell your old lady to bring in five packs of one-hundred dollar bills. The Greenleaf bank is open late on Fridays, so no excuses."

The owner cast a questioning glance at Johnny, who nodded his head indicating he should do what he was told. Then Mr. Leeds shuffled his way to the phone.

"If there's a squeak out of anyone, there's gonna be trouble. Tattoo, there, is fast with the trigger," Ferret-face warned. "And you, Baldy, tell her not to ask questions, just to do what you say."

A deathly pall pervaded the ice-cream shop, and even the small children who had been nervously crying, were frozen with fear into silence.

The owner, his hands trembling, dialed his home number. He shook all over while he waited for his wife to pick up the receiver. Then, making a super-human effort to sound normal, he told his wife to bring cash to the Tutti-Frutti. "Fifty thousand dollars, in packs of one hundred dollars."

Her response must have been bizarre, because Mr. Leeds held the phone away from his ear. Then he managed to say, "*Bring it,* honey, bring it. I'll explain later." He hung up, breathing heavily, and started to sit down on a chair near the phone.

"Okay, so far, Baldy. But before you relax, open the cash register. I can use some small bills," Ferret-face said.

Mr. Leeds walked robotlike to the cash register located at the front of the store and hit the key that opened the cash drawer. Ferret-face grabbed a fistful of bills and stuffed them into a drawstring bag that he had pulled out of his back pocket. "You can keep the change," he snickered. "But that's a nice watch you're wearing."

The owner, without a word, fumbled with his watch strap, finally unfastened it, and dropped it in the bag.

"Now you see how it's done," Ferret-face said, turning his back on Mr. Leeds who collapsed in a chair. "Everyone get their money out — don't hold anything back — and drop your jewelry in the bag. This will keep us entertained until the money arrives — or the police. If the police show up first, we've got fifteen hostages, and they'll have to negotiate."

Faith was chilled with fear, and like everyone else she didn't want to upset the holdup men. She dug in her bag for her wallet and pulled out six dollars. Then she removed her silver earrings and a Timex watch, which was all the jewelry she was wearing. As she watched Ferret-face tormenting the hostages with nasty remarks and his pointed gun, forcing them to give up their money and jewelry, she hoped desperately that the police would come. How else could they be rescued? Tattoo might shoot someone, just to show his power. *Please*, she prayed, *please*. If only the police would show up they'd have a chance. Maybe someone outside would see what's happening and call the cops.

Everyone was getting restless, especially the small children, who started whimpering.

"Shut those kids up. They're making me nervous," Ferret-face yelled at the mother, who clutched the children to her and whispered to them.

At least an hour had passed, but it seemed much longer. Tattoo began shifting his weight from one foot to the other and playfully aimed his gun at different people, saying "Bang, bang." He was a nut, and trigger happy.

Where are the police? Faith thought, *Where are they?*

"I'm getting sick of this waiting," Tattoo whined. "Why don't we pass on the big stuff, and make our getaway on the cycles right now?"

"Are you crazy, Tattoo? That's not what we came for," Ferret-face snapped. He turned to Mr. Leeds. "Your wife wouldn't ignore you, would she?"

"N — no. She knows it's important."

Just then, there was a rap on the door.

"Open it," Ferret-face barked at Tattoo. "It must be her."

Tattoo, his gun poised, slowly opened the door. A small, gray-haired woman, with a frazzled look and eyes wide with fear walked into the shop.

"Here's the money," she muttered, looking around for her husband.

"This way, lady," Ferret-face barked, and reached for the bag of money. "It better all be here."

He dumped the contents on the counter and began counting. There were five packs of hundred-dollar bills, as ordered, and the sinister grin on Ferret-face became more diabolical as he flipped through the money.

"Okay, gang, now everyone move into the back room and get down on the floor. It's time for us to split."

Ferret-face hustled the hostages into the back room at gunpoint and instructed them to lie down. Tattoo, who didn't want to miss anything, left his post at the door that he had neglected to relock, and followed them. At that instant, five policemen stormed into the store.

"Freeze!" the first policeman roared, training his gun on Ferret-face. Ferret-face turned around, petrified, and started to make a break for the window nearest him, but two policemen blocked his way and wrestled him to the ground, disarming him in the process. Meanwhile, Tattoo was so bewildered that he dropped his gun and bolted for the door. The first policeman grabbed him and forced his arms behind his back, while another cop clapped his wrists with handcuffs.

The hostages screamed with joy when they saw that their captors had been seized, hand-cuffed, and disarmed. They were manic with relief as they helped each other up from the floor.

"Close call," Johnny said to the first police officer. "How did you manage?"

"We were all set to surround the place after we received a panicky phone call from the manager of the Greenleaf bank. He said that Mrs. Leeds, acting very nervous, had asked for fifty-thousand dollars in cash. He tried to get her to talk, but she was too frightened, and just begged him to hurry, that she had to get to the ice cream store. We were sure that something was going on. This was for the big bucks, and we were sure customers were being held hostage."

Everyone was transfixed by the policeman's account of what had happened. "What then?" Faith asked, breathlessly.

"Then, without Mrs. Leeds knowing it, we followed her to the Tutti-Frutti, crept toward the windows in a crouched position, waited for her to enter, and quietly watched the proceedings. When we saw that one punk counting the money, and smiling, we knew he was ready to make his getaway. Then when he forced everyone into the back room, and his tattooed assistant followed, we were ready to pounce. What made it easy was that the door was unlocked, and we took them by surprise."

Mr. Leeds, his arm around his wife, who was quietly crying tears of relief, had regained his composure. He thanked the police for their valor, complimented the patrons of his shop for their magnificent cooperation, and singled out Johnny for his bravery. "Thanks to this young man," Mr. Leeds said, pointing to Johnny, "we kept cool. He didn't seem at all afraid."

"Nice work, kid," the first officer said. "One thing we know for sure. If the hostages start acting up, the terrorists get flakey and then they're capable of wholesale murder. What's your name, young man?"

"Johnny Bates."

"Sounds to me like you'd make a good police officer."

"Thank you, sir," Johnny said, beaming.

Then, as the officers hustled the terrorists out of the restaurant, the customers relaxed and congratulated Johnny on his quick thinking and gutsy reactions. Mr. Leeds, relieved that no one had been hurt, and that his money had been returned, said happily, "Ice-cream concoctions of your choice — on the house!"

Johnny eased away from the crowd and guided Faith toward their booth in the back. After they sat down opposite each other, Johnny reached for Faith's hand and held it in both of his. "You're the only one who hasn't said anything to me," he said.

After a moment's silence, she responded. "Johnny," she began slowly, "you were wonderful. I thought we might all be killed by those madmen. And I have a confession."

"A confession?"

"My whole life passed by as I watched those guys. I'd never been more scared. I knew that if the money wasn't delivered or if it wasn't all there, someone might be killed. All I kept hoping for was that the police would come. I kept thinking, 'Where are the police?' What I guess I realized is someone has to be a cop . . . someone has to be there in an emergency."

"And . . ." Johnny said.

"And . . . I guess I was wrong. I mean if you want to be a cop, okay, I'll bear it."

"That means more to me than anything else," Johnny said.

He squeezed her hand in his and neither of them said anything. Then the owner, unaware that he was interrupting, strode over to their booth.

"What'll it be, kids? You can have anything you want."

"We've already got it," Johnny said. "Right, Faith?"

"Right," she smiled, not taking her eyes off Johnny.

The owner looked at each of them, shrugged his shoulders, and walked off. "Free ice cream," he mumbled, "and they're not interested. Kids . . . I'll never understand 'em."

CHAPTER FIFTEEN

Faith had never felt so good about life. Not only had the ice-cream parlor scene convinced her that Johnny was doing the right thing in pursuing a career as a detective, but for the first time she could understand her father's dedication to his work. She'd been operating in slow motion, going about her work in a halfhearted way. Now she felt she could climb Mt. Everest.

She hadn't even bothered to develop the film that she and Mary Beth had taken. Tracy had already asked her three times what was taking so long, and Faith had made some feeble excuses.

On Saturday she found Tracy at breakfast and promised that she would work on the film that day.

"It's about time," Tracy snapped. "I was about to give up on you."

"Don't blame you," Faith said, mildly. She was used to Tracy's manner and was not put off by her in the least.

Faith looked around for Mary Beth, but it wasn't until she returned to Baker that she saw her coming out of the dorm, dressed in a skirt and shirt, carrying a tote bag. Mary Beth had been so somber lately, almost as withdrawn as she had been in the early days of school.

"Hi, M.B.," Faith greeted her. "I've been looking for you. Tracy's bugging me about the *Clarion* pictures, and I promised we'd develop the film today."

"Can't," Mary Beth said sullenly. "I'm visiting my father today."

"That's good." Faith, who was feeling so happy, wanted desperately to cheer up Mary Beth. "Do you want me to wait till you get back and we can work together?"

"I don't really care," she muttered. "I don't really care about anything anymore."

"Come on," Faith pleaded, "nothing's really changed."

"That's the trouble."

"What about Richard? You said you really like him, and he obviously liked you."

"I do like him, but he doesn't know my father's in prison and that most of Canby Hall thinks I'm a thief."

"If you explained everything, he'd understand."

"But what if he doesn't? Better I shouldn't see him."

"M.B., please. You've got to give him a chance. . . ."

Mary Beth backed away. "I've got to go now, or I'll miss the bus. I hope we got some good shots."

Faith watched Mary Beth until she was out of sight, wishing more than ever that she could help her, but she was discouraged. As her roommates had suggested, she had asked Johnny's advice about how to find the real thief, told him how the whole school was alerted, and what Miss Allardyce had said at assembly. Faith's conversation took place with Johnny shortly after the holdup, and she fully expected him to come up with some magic solution. But after listening carefully, he said, "The number of unsolved crimes is mind-boggling. I'm afraid this one might just add to the statistic."

Faith couldn't hide her disappointment, but realistically she knew he was probably right.

It's not fair, it's not fair, Faith thought as she went up the stairs to her room.

She took the rolls of film out of her desk drawer and walked over to the darkroom, which was just opposite the *Clarion* office. She glanced into the office where there was an unusual amount of activity for a Saturday. It was clear that the entire staff was feeling the pressure of getting the issue out on time, and tempers were frayed. The features editor was arguing with the managing editor about needing more space for her article on graduation, the art editor was complaining about the lack of imagination in the layout, one of the reporters was in tears because her feature story had been cut in half, and Mr. Bowker was trying to smooth everyone's ruffled feathers.

Faith wanted to keep out of the way and immediately ducked into the darkroom, where she stood blinking for a full minute. When her eyes had gotten accustomed to the darkness, and she was about to prepare the developing solutions, she heard Tracy's sharp voice.

"Millie," she barked, "don't you know not to unroll the film *before* you're in the dark-room?"

"But somebody's in there. There's that red light flashing on the door that says 'in use.' You said you were in a hurry for these pictures, so I thought I'd get a head start."

"I don't believe you're for real. You asked for more responsibility, you told me you knew how to develop film, and now you've exposed the entire roll."

"It was just some shots I took on Parent's Day. You said I wasn't the only one taking them, so you must have others."

"Fortunately," Tracy rasped. "But that's not the point."

"What is the point, then?" Millie asked.

"The point is, Millie, you can't do anything right."

"That's not true." Millie, for the first time, sounded personally insulted. "I can do a lot right."

"Like what?" Tracy asked.

"Like put things over on people, without them knowing it."

"What's that supposed to mean?" Tracy asked.

"I'm good at surprising people, that's what."

"You'd surprise me if that roll of film came out now." Tracy couldn't resist getting in a last dig.

"I make mistakes, but I am good at fooling everyone."

"Look, Millie, I don't know what you're talking about, and I don't have time now to find out. I've got a million things to do."

Faith thought Tracy must have started to walk away because she could hear Millie call after her. "Come back, and I'll tell you something nobody knows."

"What?" Tracy asked impatiently. "What am I about to be let in on?"

Millie was breathing so hard that Faith could hear her through the closed door, and she knew Millie was screwing up her courage.

Faith held her breath as she waited for Millie's announcement.

"I'm the one who stole things from Baker and nobody knew it," Millie said evenly.

"You what?" Tracy gasped.

"Yeah, it was me and nobody guessed." Millie was obviously proud of her achievement.

Faith was stunned. She couldn't believe her ears. Her hands got sweaty and her heart began pumping wildly, and she burst out of the darkroom to make sure she wasn't hallucinating.

"Did I hear you right, Millie? Did you steal things from our dorm?" Faith asked.

"I did," she replied. Faith was amazed at how unperturbed she appeared.

"What did you take?" Tracy, like Faith, was shocked by Millie's confession and wanted to make sure her ears weren't deceiving her.

"I stole Shelley's bangles, Cheryl's blouse, Ginny's sweater, Ellie's locket, and Maggie's violin," Millie bragged.

"But why?" Faith asked. Faith was glad that Mary Beth's name would be cleared, but she couldn't help feeling sorry for Millie.

"Just to show that I could," Millie replied.

"Were you planning to use any of the things, or sell them?" Tracy asked.

"Of course not, I don't need them. They're all in my bottom drawer, and I wasn't even going to bother taking them home."

"Then why, Millie? Why did you do it?" Faith asked gently.

Millie looked her straight in the eye and then said tearfully, her bravado suddenly disappearing, "Because everybody's better than I am, and I wanted to do something special."

Faith bit her lip, and tried not to show how desperately sorry she felt for Millie. Tracy, too, was at a loss for words, and a look of pain crossed her face.

Finally Faith said, "Millie, it's good that you finally told us about this."

Tracy, taking her cue from Faith, spoke with uncharacteristic softness. "Faith's right, Millie. It's not good to keep everything bottled up inside you."

Millie, unable to speak, wept silently, the tears streaming down her face.

Faith darted into the darkroom and came out with a paper towel, which she handed to Millie to use as a tissue. Millie wiped away her tears, and Faith took her arm.

"Come on, Millie. We'll go see Alison. She'll know what to do," Faith said.

They shepherded her out of the building, back to Baker, and up to Alison's "penthouse."

Alison had just gotten out of the shower when they arrived and had slipped on a terry cloth robe to answer the door. Her wet hair was wrapped in a towel like a turban, but she didn't seem the least bit perturbed by the unexpected visit.

"Come in, come in," she welcomed them in her usual friendly manner. Then, seeing Millie's bloodshot eyes, and the other girls' unsmiling faces, she knew there was trouble.

"We're glad we caught you," Faith said.

"What's happened?" Alison asked.

Then Millie, who had stopped crying on the way over, was suddenly overcome with a fresh flood of tears. She thrust her arms around Alison and wept openly, while Alison said nothing and held her for several minutes until she quieted down.

"I did it," Millie said between sniffles. "I'm the thief everyone's been looking for."

Alison, with remarkable calm, said, "It's taken a lot of courage for you to admit this, Millie."

"It has?" Millie was astonished and pushed herself away so that she could see Alison's face. As though a crisis had passed, the girls who had been standing flopped down on the floor pillows.

"I'm going to return everything anyway. I didn't want any of that stuff," Millie said.

"Millie, some of those things meant a lot to their owners," Tracy said.

"And didn't mean anything to me. I don't care a thing about clothes, and I can't even play the violin."

They all had to laugh at that, and even Millie relaxed.

"What'll happen to me now, Alison?" Millie asked.

"We'll have to tell your parents," Alison said.

"That doesn't matter. They're always traveling someplace and couldn't care less about me. I was sent to boarding school when I was ten, and every summer since I was six, I've gone to camp."

"Oh no," Faith said, sympathetically.

"What about Miss Allardyce? Do you have to tell her?" Millie looked frightened.

"Yes," Alison replied, "but she cares very much about every girl at Canby Hall, and she'll do everything she can to help you."

"Like send me to reform school?" Millie asked.

"Never," Alison assured her. "But she'll make sure you'll get some counseling, and next year — now that you've made this giant step in helping yourself — I know life will be much better for you."

"I hope so," Millie said. "It couldn't get much worse."

"You'll see, you'll be happier," Alison told her.

Millie had a faraway look in her eyes, and as though she were talking to herself, she muttered, "That's the first nice thing anyone's said to me the whole year."

*   *   *

It was five o'clock in the afternoon and Faith, Shelley, and Dana were in a state of borderline hysteria waiting for Mary Beth's return. The girls were sorry that Millie had suffered so much without them ever taking notice of her. But they couldn't help being overjoyed that she had confessed.

Alison had arranged for all the stolen items to be returned, and saved Millie from the embarrassment of facing the girls she had victimized. Then she took Millie to the head-mistress's house, and as Alison predicted, Miss Allardyce was much more interested in helping Millie than in punishing her. Alison, who knew that talk of Millie's confession was traveling across the campus like wildfire, told a few key people the results of the meeting with the headmistress. She wanted to squelch the rumors and speculations that Millie was going to be expelled from school, not allowed to return next year, or forced to make a public apology. The truth was, Millie had to agree to see a therapist on a regular basis, and since she had been guilty of stealing had to be grounded for the remaining school year.

Mary Beth was not feeling at all sociable, and quietly climbed the stairs, hoping no one would notice her. She couldn't avoid passing room 407, and since the door was open she waved perfunctorily and hurried by.

"Come here, M.B.!" Shelley yelled.

"Later," Mary Beth said, as she continued down the hall.

"No, now!" Dana insisted, sticking her head out the door. "We've got something to tell you."

"It can wait," Mary Beth mumbled, without looking back.

"No, it can't," Dana called.

Then Shelley raced down the hall and literally yanked Mary Beth back to their room and closed the door.

"What's going on?" Mary Beth asked, sensing that something monumental had happened.

"The mystery's been solved," Dana exclaimed gleefully.

"What?" Mary Beth breathed, and sank down on Dana's bed near the door, trying to comprehend the news.

"Millie confessed," Dana went on. "And all the stolen goods have been returned."

"Which means there's no way anybody can accuse you of anything, ever," Shelley added, rather ridiculously.

"I can't believe it. I just can't believe it. But how, why, what did she do it for?" Mary Beth asked.

Faith described how she overheard Tracy's conversation with Millie outside the darkroom, and all that had transpired after that.

Mary Beth sighed. "I guess Millie couldn't help how she behaved. But thank goodness she confessed. I was beginning to feel like . . ."

"Never mind how you were beginning to feel," Dana interrupted. "That's all behind you now."

"That's one thing I don't have to worry about telling Richard, but he still doesn't know about my father."

"Nobody thinks about that anymore, M.B.," Shelley said.

"That's because they're used to the idea, but Richard still doesn't know."

"Richard *does* know," Dana said.

"He knows?" Mary Beth was shocked. "Then why didn't he say anything?"

"I guess he was waiting for you to bring it up. He told Bret he couldn't care less about your father."

Mary Beth grinned self-consciously, and then looked at her friends. "Thanks to you," she said, "I'll never have to worry about being a girl with a secret again." She waved at them absentmindedly and left their room, wanting to be alone for a while.

Dana, Shelley, and Faith were silent for a few minutes, too. Then Dana said, "Well we've certainly been through a lot together this year. Haven't we?"

Shelley nodded. "Three new boyfriends — one each. That must be a record of some kind. Not to mention a kidnapping."

Faith laughed. "And you and I not exactly getting along at the beginning of the year."

"Talk about not getting along, Shelley and I sure had our battles a couple of months ago," Dana added.

"Nobody mentioned when I got caught almost cheating on an exam," Shelley said.

"But you didn't cheat," Dana said quickly.

The girls looked at each other affectionately. "I guess that's what good friendships are all about," Dana said thoughtfully. "Surviving a lot of trouble together."

"We sure did that," Faith agreed.

"Enough," Dana said, jumping up from her bed. "Who's for the Tutti-Frutti? Treat's on me!"

"Where are you going to get the money from?" Faith asked.

"Easy," Dana said, "I'm going to borrow it from my two best friends. After all, what are best friends for?"

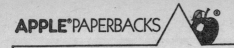